Praise for the bestselling and award-winning *Julius Zebra* series

"AN
IRREVERENT,
FAST-PACED AND ZANY
INTRODUCTION TO ROMAN BRITAIN ...
EDUCATIONAL AND
HILARIOUS!"
SOUTH WALES EVENING POST

"...A
COMPLETELY
LUDICROUS
AND HILARIOUS STORY PACKED
WITH CARTOON PICTURES"
NEWBURY WEEKLY NEWS

"FUNNY,
WITTY AND
OUTRAGEOUS"
THE SCHOOL LIBRARIAN

"A
PLEASINGLY
DAFT ROMP ...
HAS A VERY HORRIBLE
HISTORIES SENSE OF HUMOUR"
FINANCIAL TIMES

"BONKERS,
FAST-PACED AND
FUNNY ... A
ROMAN
ROLLERCOASTER
OF A RIDE"
PHILIP ARDAGH

"...A BRILLIANT MIX OF
HISTORICAL
FACT AND
SILLY
FICTION"
SUNDAY EXPRESS

"THIS
EXCITING
BOOK MADE ME
LAUGH
OUT LOUD!"
NATIONAL GEOGRAPHIC KIDS

JULIUS ZEBRA

ENTANGLED WITH THE EGYPTIANS!

GARY NORTHFIELD

**WALKER
BOOKS**

For my brilliant editor Lizzie,
thank you for ten years of
boundless enthusiasm and patience!
(Ten years?! Flippin' eck!)

Special thanks to Chloe for taking
all this nonsense in her stride.

First published in Great Britain 2017 by Walker Books Ltd
87 Vauxhall Walk, London SE11 5HJ

2 4 6 8 10 9 7 5 3 1

© 2017 Gary Northfield

The right of Gary Northfield to be identified as author and illustrator
of this work has been asserted by him in accordance with the
Copyright, Designs and Patents Act 1988

This book has been typeset in Stempel Schneidler

Printed and bound in Great Britain by CPI Group (UK) Ltd, Croydon CR0 4YY

British Library Cataloguing in Publication Data:
a catalogue record for this book is available from the British Library

ISBN 978-1-4063-7180-2

www.walker.co.uk

CONTENTS

So you think you know about

JULIUS ZEBRA?

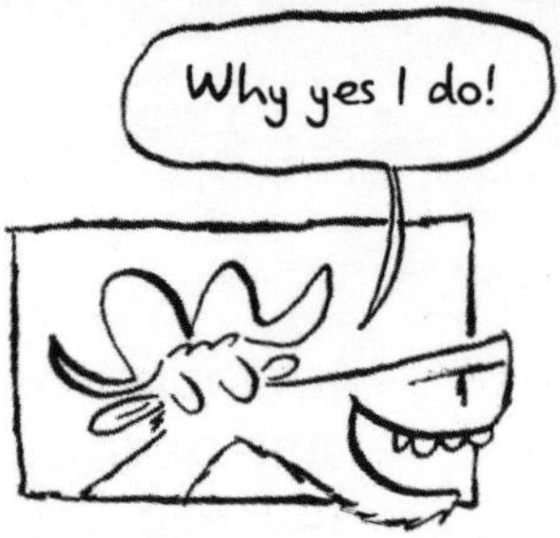
Why yes I do!

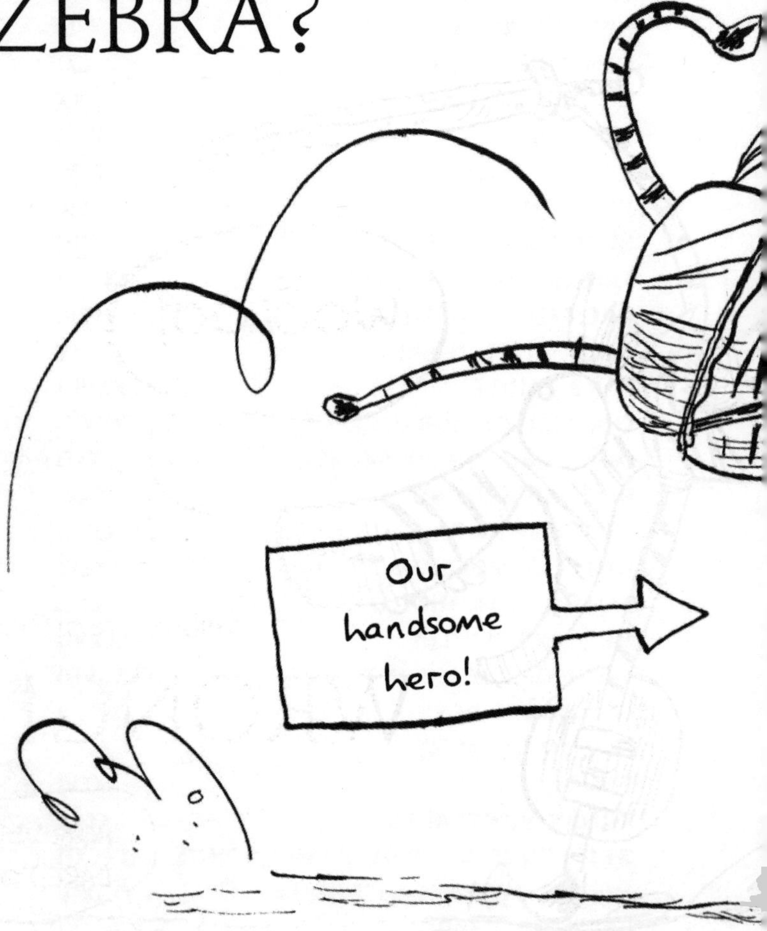
Our handsome hero!

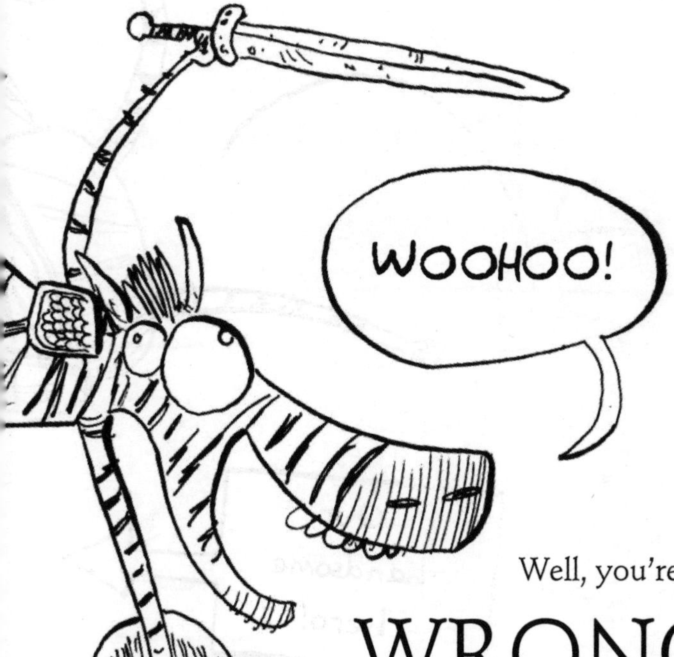
WOOHOO!

Well, you're probably

WRONG!

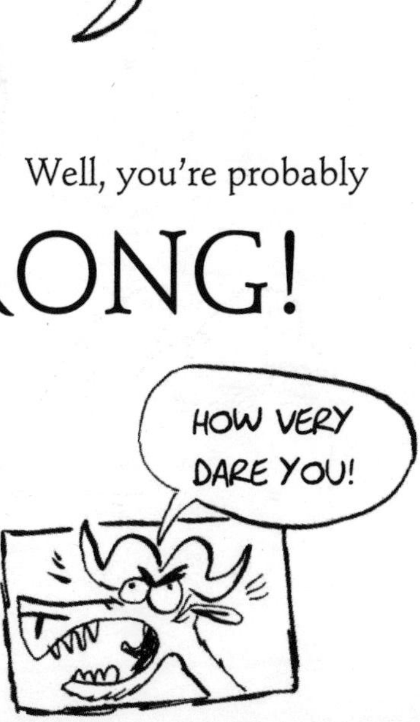
HOW VERY DARE YOU!

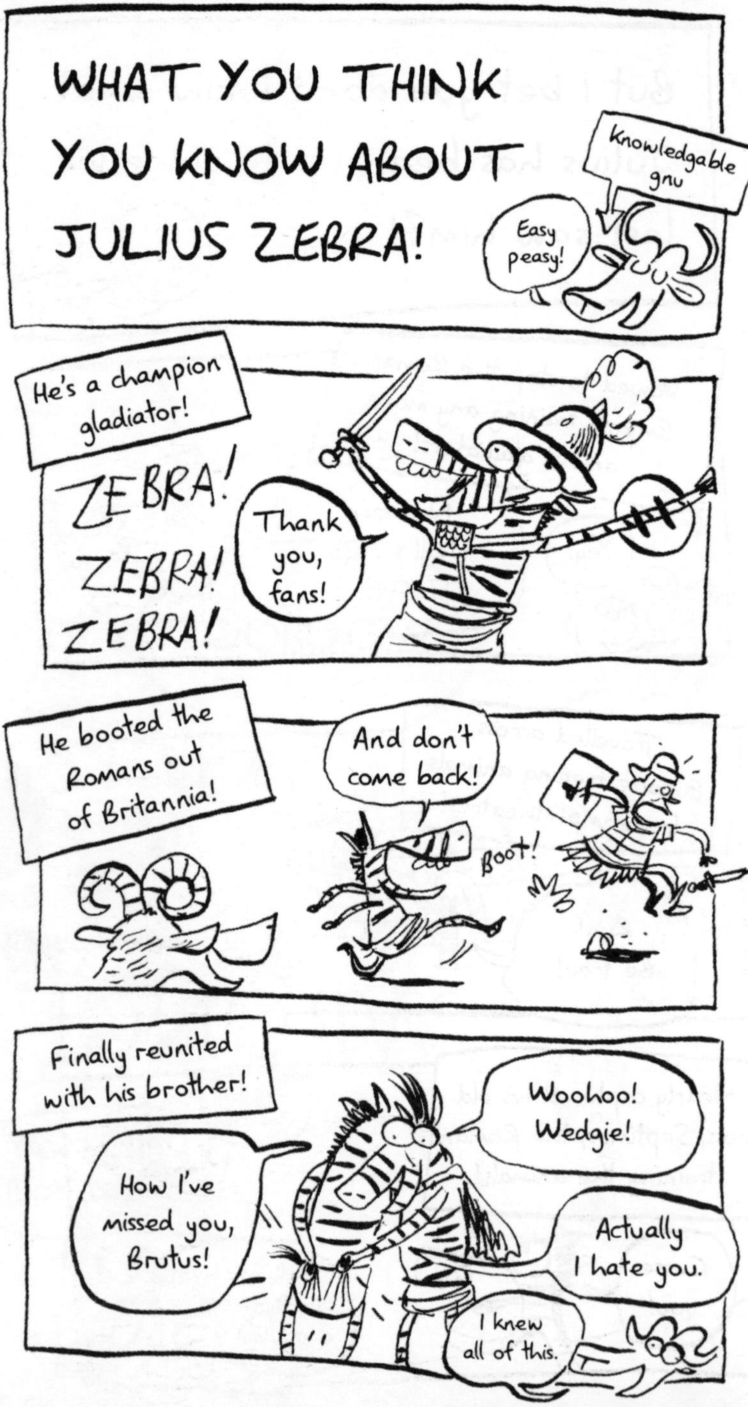
WHAT YOU THINK YOU KNOW ABOUT JULIUS ZEBRA!
Knowledgable gnu
Easy peasy!
He's a champion gladiator!
ZEBRA! ZEBRA! ZEBRA!
Thank you, fans!
He booted the Romans out of Britannia!
And don't come back!
Boot!
Finally reunited with his brother!
Woohoo! Wedgie!
How I've missed you, Brutus!
Actually I hate you.
I knew all of this.

But I bet you don't know what Julius has been up to since we last saw him?!

This I gotta see.

Vowed to stop the Roman Empire training any more animal gladiators!

Yay!

No more shall we be SLAVES!

Travelled across Europe freeing animals from amphitheatres!

Oi!

Hooray!

Run! Be free!

Nearly captured his old boss, Septimus, the Roman training the animals!

See ya losers!

Curse you!

Well, you learn something new every day!

Julius wasn't like other zebras and he was determined to prove it!

Exciting, right?

CHAPTER ONE
SHIP OF FOOLS

"YES!" cried Cornelius, as he desperately stood on his tiptoes grasping the wet tiller. "JUST HOLD THE BIG STICK STEADY!"

Julius wiped the blinding rain from his eyes. "BUT I'M SURE WE'RE GOING ROUND IN CIRCLES!" he shouted. "DOUBLE-CHECK THOSE INSTRUCTIONS AGAIN!"

With a huff, Cornelius reached into the pouch tied round his waist and pulled out a crumpled scrap of parchment. The soggy note flapped furiously in the wind as he struggled to read it.

"WE'RE DOING EXACTLY WHAT IT SAYS!" Cornelius called out. "'HOLD THE TILLER STEADY IN A HEAVY STORM'!"

But, just as Cornelius held his note proudly aloft, a great gust of wind snatched it from his hoof and tossed it into the sea.

"Oh, that's just brilliant," groaned Julius.

"FORGET SEPTIMUS! WE SHOULD TURN AROUND!" Cornelius squealed. "OR ELSE THIS STORM WILL SWALLOW US WHOLE!"

But Julius was having none of it. "Wait here!" he growled through gritted teeth, pulling himself along the deck. "HOLD HER STEADY, CORNELIUS! I'M FETCHING HELP!"

A huge wave crashed against the side and Julius stumbled as he headed towards the captain's cabin. He reached the open hatch and, grabbing hold of the slippery ladder, he climbed down gingerly into the dank, dark underbelly of the ship.

In the gloom, Julius pushed past Milus the lion, who was lying in a tatty hammock. On his belly gently slept Pliny the mouse, their tiny combat trainer. Displeased at being woken, Milus growled at Julius.

"No, we're not!" snapped Julius. "And the way things are looking, we'll never get there."

Julius clambered over a pile of soggy crates and sacks, where he finally found the rest of his companions huddled in a circle.

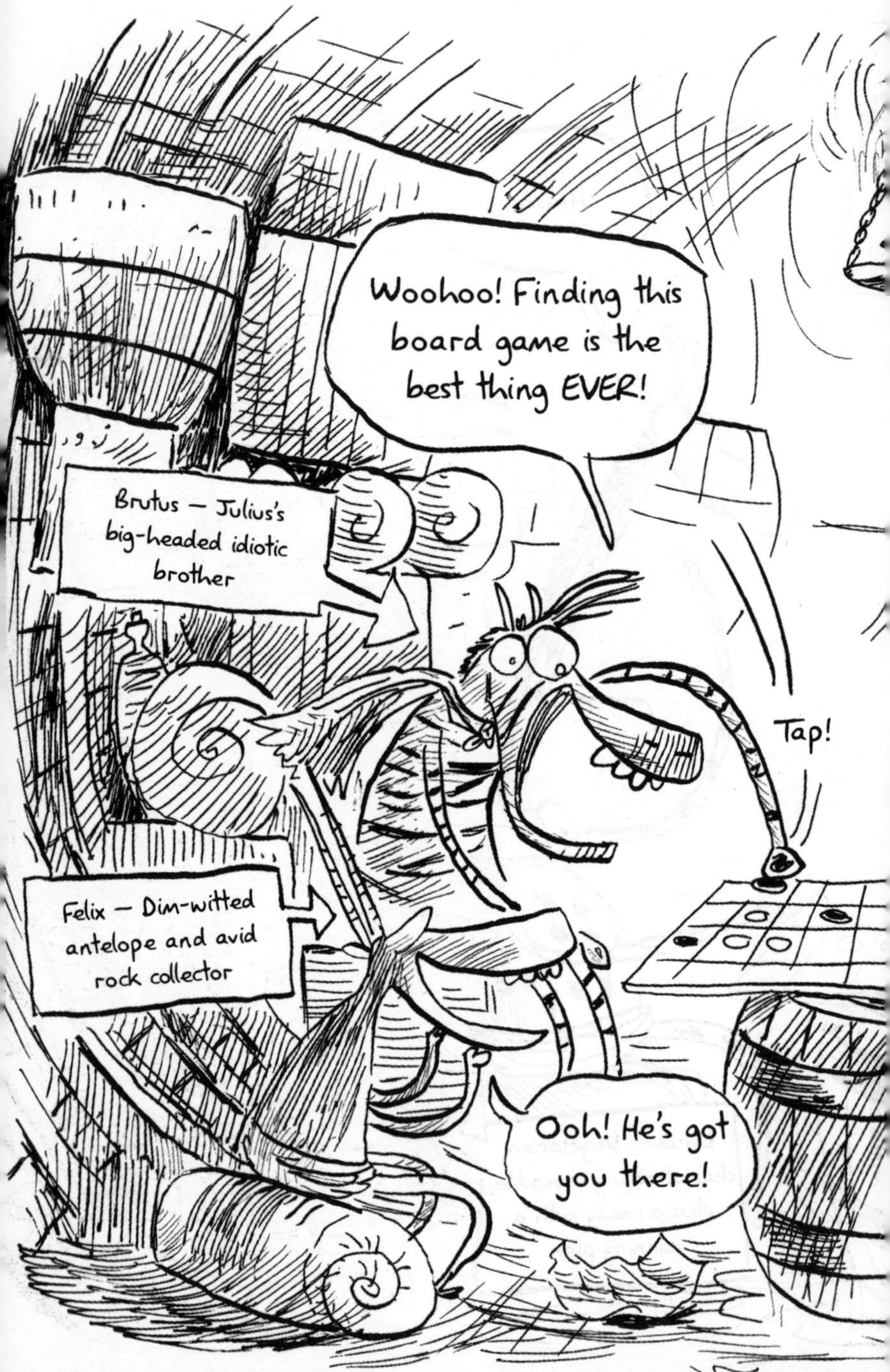

Woohoo! Finding this board game is the best thing EVER!
Brutus – Julius's big-headed idiotic brother
Tap!
Felix – Dim-witted antelope and avid rock collector
Ooh! He's got you there!

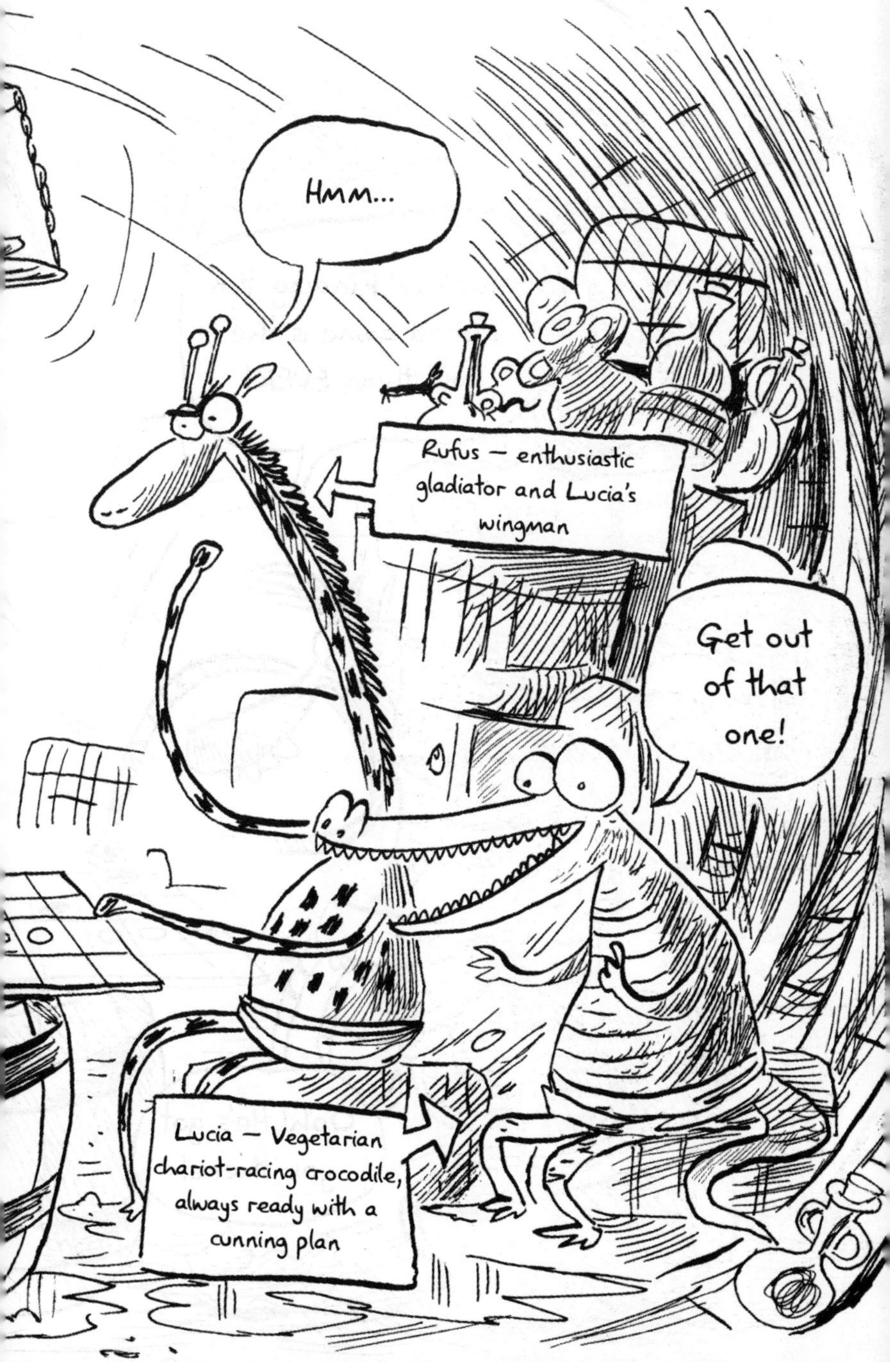
HMM...
Rufus – enthusiastic gladiator and Lucia's wingman
Get out of that one!
Lucia – Vegetarian chariot-racing crocodile, always ready with a cunning plan

Everyone jumped out of their skins, apart from his brother, Brutus, who refused to look up. "You'll have to wait, Julius!" he growled. "This is a very tense match!" He waved his hoof to shoo his brother away.

Rufus, Lucia and Felix all leapt up in horror. "WHAT?!" they screamed.

"I thought the ship was swaying a bit," gasped Felix. "It's been hard work trying to watch the game!"

Before Julius could reply, there was a great BANG as the ship buckled and twisted under the force of an enormous wave. It tipped over sideways, hurling everyone and all the cargo into the air.

The ship quickly righted itself, but Julius knew another big wave could hit at any moment and rip the old ship apart. He hurried up the wet ladder. "COME ON! WE NEED TO GET THIS SHIP THROUGH THE STORM!"

Suddenly Lucia started screaming. "WE'RE LETTING IN WATER! WE'RE LETTING IN WATER!" She pointed frantically at a big leak spurting water.

"YOU, RUFUS AND MILUS BLOCK THAT HOLE!" ordered Julius. "THE REST OF YOU, FOLLOW ME!"

Climbing out of the hatch, Julius raced over to poor Cornelius, who was still wrestling with the big tiller.

Lucia and Julius leapt onto the big stick and held it as steadily as possible. "GRAB THE OTHER ONE AND HOLD IT!" yelled Julius to Felix and Brutus, who quickly ran to the other side of the boat and grasped the second flailing tiller.

As the rain lashed down from pitch-black clouds, the sea looked like a crazy mountain range thrusting high into the sky, before crashing back down into swirling chasms.

The wind screamed as it ripped through the sail, dragging the ship from one frightening lunge to another.

We need to get that sail down before it pulls us under!

"BUT HOW?!" cried Julius.

Suddenly the great gale whipped through the ship, sweeping the stricken vessel high up on a mountainous wave. There was a loud CRACKING noise as the sail was buffeted out as if fit to burst.

"LOOK OUT!" screamed Brutus, as the heavy ropes that held the sail to the ship pinged off like they were mere washing lines.

With another frightening CRACK the mast and sail were torn off into the raging turmoil of storm clouds.

Well, that's sorted THAT problem out!

Then, at that moment, Cornelius looked past Julius, the blood draining from his little face. "I – I think it might just be the BEGINNING of our problems!" he squeaked, pointing upwards.

Julius turned to see a monstrous wall of water rising and blocking out the sky.

"C-can you swim, Julius?" stuttered Cornelius.

"We'll soon find out!" he gulped. And he held his breath, squeezed his eyes shut and clung on to the tiller for dear life.

CHAPTER TWO
BEACHED WAILS

Julius was woken by a voice calling his name.
He blinked open his eyes to find a familiar face
staring at him.

Julius groaned. His ribs were bruised and he had a
very sore head. Cold water sloshed around his legs.
Then he heard more voices calling his name and the
splish-sploshing of paddling hooves.

Squinting from the dazzling sun, Julius opened his eyes a little wider.

Julius slowly pulled himself up, wincing at his aches and pains. "Where ... where are we?" he murmured. He looked around the beach, shielding his eyes from the sun with his hoof. Strewn across the golden, sandy shore were broken crates, smashed jugs, twisted rope and hundreds of pieces of wood of all shapes and sizes. In the sea even more fragments were floating idly on the tide. The familiar figures of Brutus, Pliny and Milus were picking through the debris.

"We're alive!" gasped Julius. "Somehow we're alive!"

"That was quite the storm!" said Cornelius chirpily. "And it seems the gods were on our side, as we were fortunate enough to be near land as it hit!"

Julius finally stood up, stretched his back and again looked around the beach. He took in a deep breath, the hot air burning his nostrils.

"Cor!" he blurted out. "Now there's a smell I haven't smelt in a VERY long time!" Kneeling, he sniffed a big rock and let out a big jolly gasp of air.

Then he grabbed a big hoof-ful of shrubs and gave them a big sniff too.

"Can it be true: are we home?"

"That's a very good question!" replied Cornelius. "In fact, we've been having quite a debate about it. I'm pretty sure we're in Africa!"

He scampered off ahead round some big sand dunes. "Follow me!"

"Where are you going?" asked Julius, his achy legs barely able to carry him.

"Lucia's got something to show you!" announced the warthog.

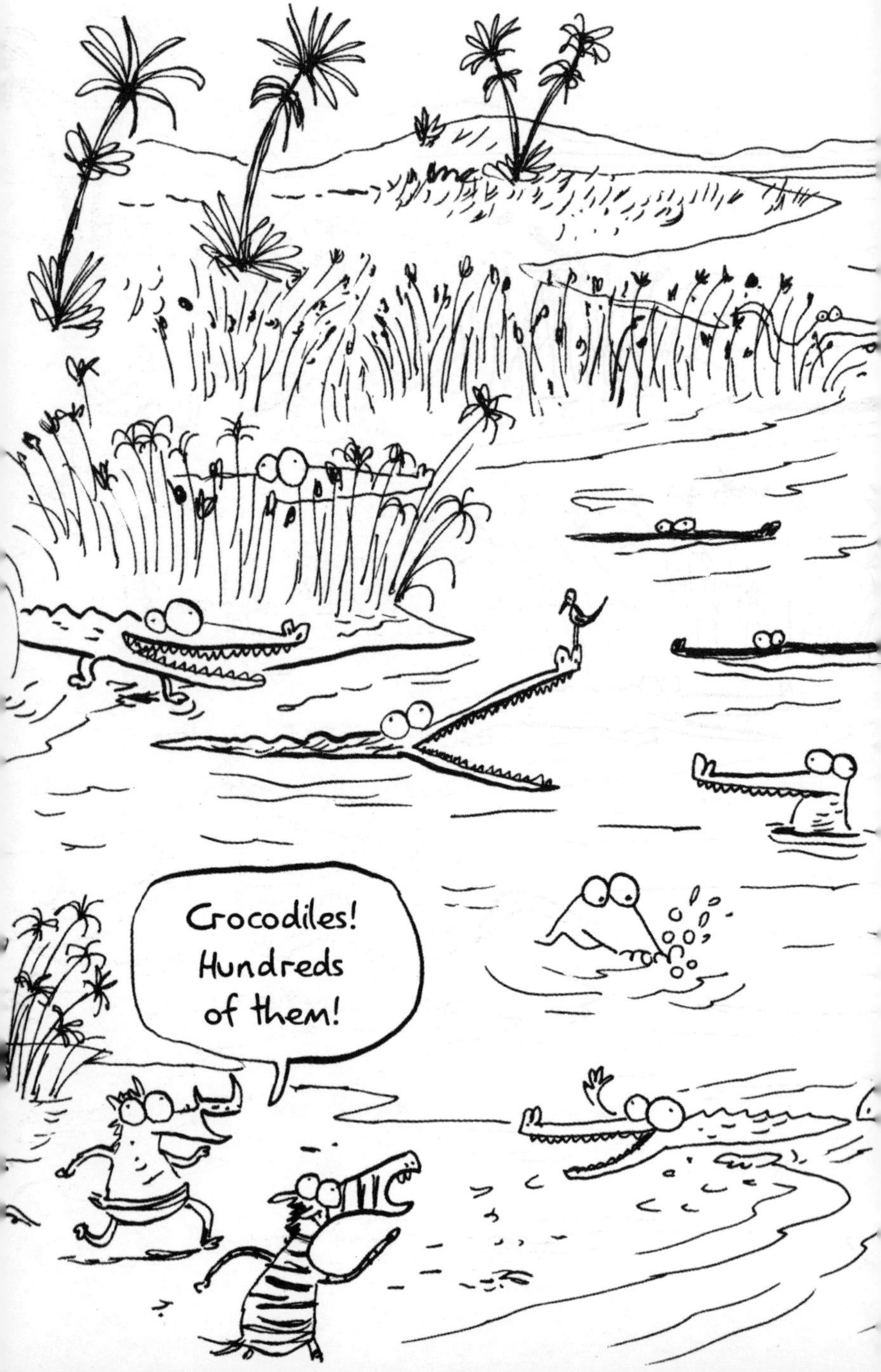
Crocodiles!
Hundreds
of them!

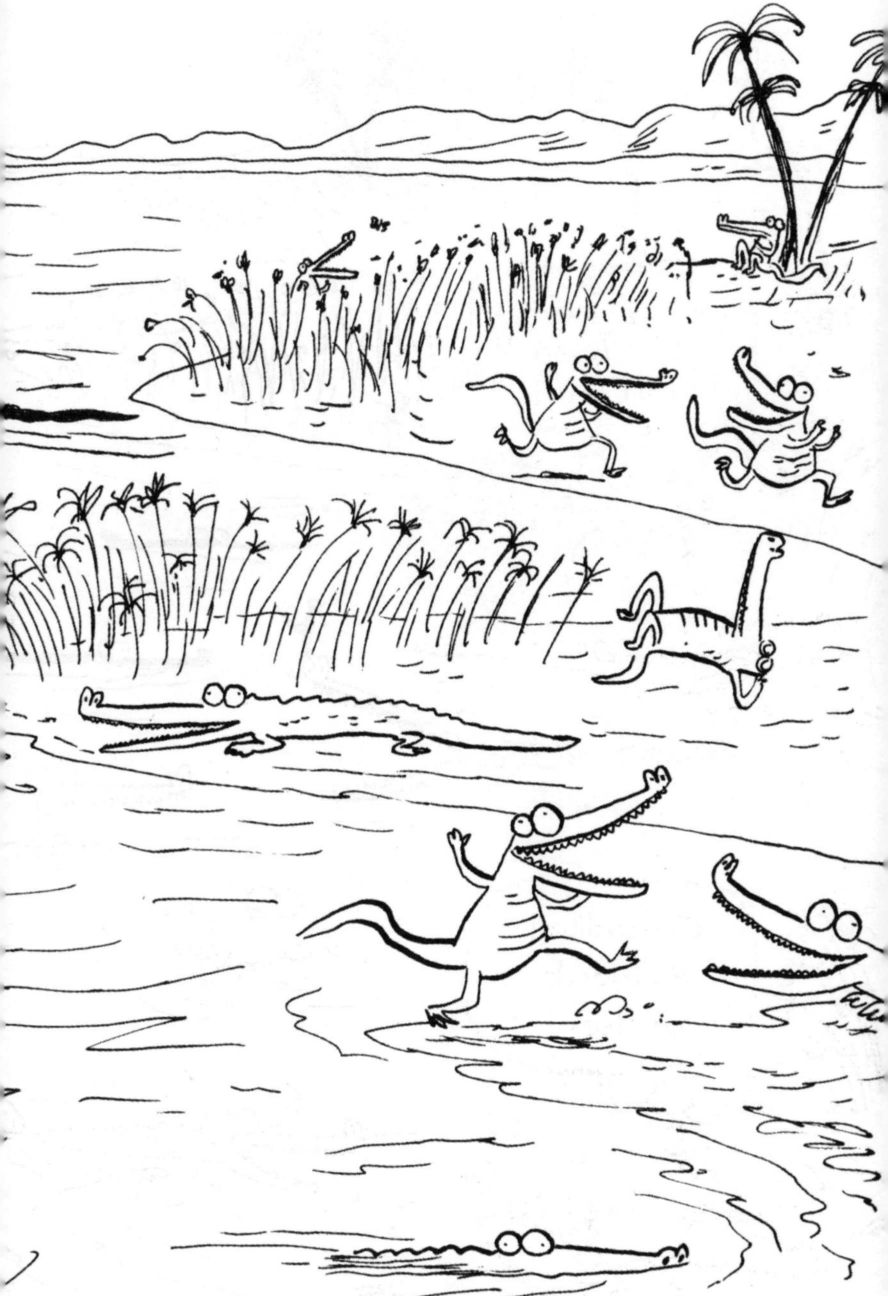

"JULIUS!" cried Lucia. She dashed over to her old friend and gave him a big hug. "We thought we'd lost you!"

Isn't it wonderful to be back in AFRICA!

"We can go HOME!" she sang gleefully.

"How can you be so sure?" exclaimed Julius.

"Well, where ELSE do you find so many crocodiles?"

Milus strode up to Julius and patted him on the shoulder. "So, donkey, even though it's been wonderful hanging out with the likes of a zebra and an antelope, it's time I left," he growled.

"But you can't leave us now, Milus!" pleaded Julius.

"We still need to find Septimus and stop him training any more animals!"

"If you think Septimus survived that storm," said Milus, walking off, "then you're a bigger fool than you look!"

"Which means we can get our lives back again," said Milus. "Goodbye."

Julius called over to Pliny the mouse, who was hopping through the flotsam of the shipwreck. "PLINY! CAN'T YOU HAVE A WORD?"

Pliny threw his paws up in despair. "Don't ya think I tried?" he squeaked. "Ain't nothing going to change his mind!"

"You know," Julius sighed, "even though he kept calling me a donkey, I think I'm going to miss the old grump."

"Very nice, Brutus! But that doesn't help with finding Septimus."

Lucia patted Julius's shoulder. "Forget Septimus," she said kindly. "Milus is right: he's either lost at sea, or shipwrecked who knows where." She gave Julius a big smile. "We're finally FREE to do whatever we want!"

"Come on, Debra!" Pliny squeaked. "We can chillax, check out the local landmarks!" He started darting about in the sand, throwing shapes and cartwheeling.

Felix ran across the beach. "Don't worry, Julius!" he shouted. "I'm not going anywhere, not when there are lots of amazing rocks to collect!"

"Yeah, you're right," laughed Julius. "In fact, thinking about it, I'm glad to see the back of Milus. If I never see him again, it will be too soon!"

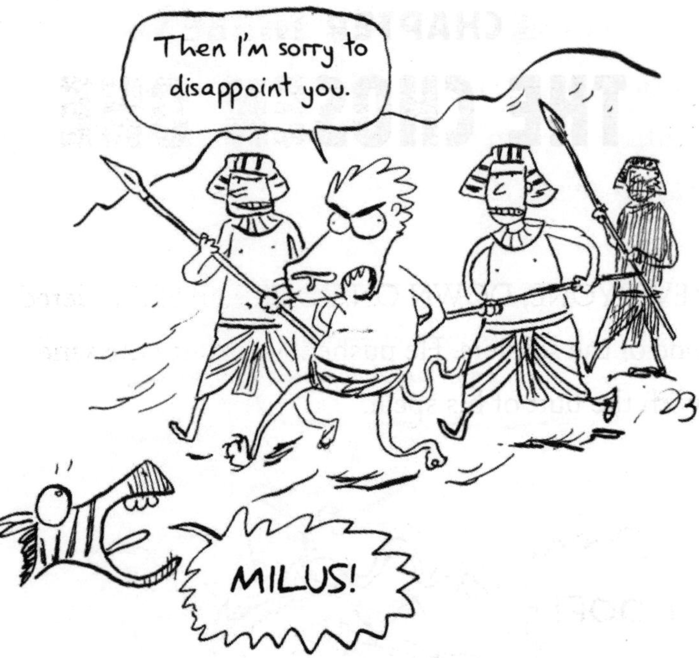
Then I'm sorry to disappoint you.
MILUS!

CHAPTER THREE

THE CHOSEN ONE

"EVERYONE, DOWN ON YOUR KNEES!" ordered one of the soldiers. He pushed Milus into the sand with the butt of his spear.

The soldier, who was obviously in command, stepped forward to examine the strange animals, his red and white striped headpiece flapping in the wind. He prodded Julius with his spear.

"Who are you that enters our land UNINVITED?" he barked.

One of the other soldiers called out from behind, "And what a mess you've made of our beach!"

All the other soldiers nodded and grumbled in agreement.

The commander leant in towards Julius, "Yes," he rasped, "and what a horrible mess you have made of our beautiful beach."

"Look, we're sorry about your beach," said Julius, "but we arrived here by accident. We were SHIPWRECKED!"

"PAH!" the commander scoffed, forcing Julius to the ground. "A likely story! You are SPIES, and in Egypt we KILL all spies!"

Cornelius slapped his forehead. "EGYPT! Of course! I knew it!"

"No, you didn't!" retorted Julius crossly. "You said *Africa*!"

"Egypt is IN Africa!" corrected Cornelius. "So I think you'll find I WAS right!"

"I'm with Julius," interjected Felix. "You can't take credit just by saying a whole CONTINENT; that's cheating!"

"I think you'll find it WAS a competition!" Felix said indignantly. "I personally said we were in Greece and Rufus said we were in Carthage. We ALL had a go!"

"Well, if it was a competition," agreed Cornelius, "what was the prize, hmm?"

Felix looked blank for a moment. "Er ... a starfish?"

"You've just MADE that UP!" protested Cornelius.

WILL YOU ALL BE QUIET!

"I don't know where you spies are from," thundered the commander, "but it must be a land full of IDIOTS!!!"

"Actually, Mr Soldier, sir," said Julius, "we're not idiots from Idiotland; we are GLADIATORS, FUGITIVES from ROME!"

The soldiers nearly choked.

"Yeah, and you'd better not mess with this one," added Cornelius, pointing at Julius. "He's their world-famous CHAMPION!"

The commander wiped a tear from his eye. "That is possibly the funniest joke I have ever heard, beast. I am going to be VERY sorry when we have to kill you."

Julius quickly grabbed two big sticks and adopted an attacking stance.

The commander stepped back, shocked and wide-eyed.

"Good work!" whispered Cornelius. "You've caught them off guard!"

The commander shook his head in disbelief. "No, no! Don't be RIDICULOUS! He couldn't possibly be..."

He didn't complete his sentence; instead he narrowed his eyes and thrust his spear at the zebra. "For a horse, you are either very brave, or very, very stupid," he spat.

"Oh, don't YOU start! I'm not a horse; I'm a—" But, before Julius could finish, he became aware of the ground shuddering underfoot. Startled, he quickly spun round.

Julius waved them away. "No, it's OK, thank you," he said gratefully. "This isn't anything I can't handle!"

The crocodiles bowed dutifully and stood back as requested.

See how he commands the crocodilus!

The frightened soldiers were flabbergasted.

"Who are you that enters our lands, bears the symbols of our long-dead pharaohs and commands the crocodiles?" cried one of them.

"Look," Julius said, raising his arms. "I just want everything to be cool!" And he gave them a big friendly smile.

Suddenly, as if on cue, dark storm clouds gathered overhead, there was a crack of thunder and the skies opened with a huge downpour of rain.

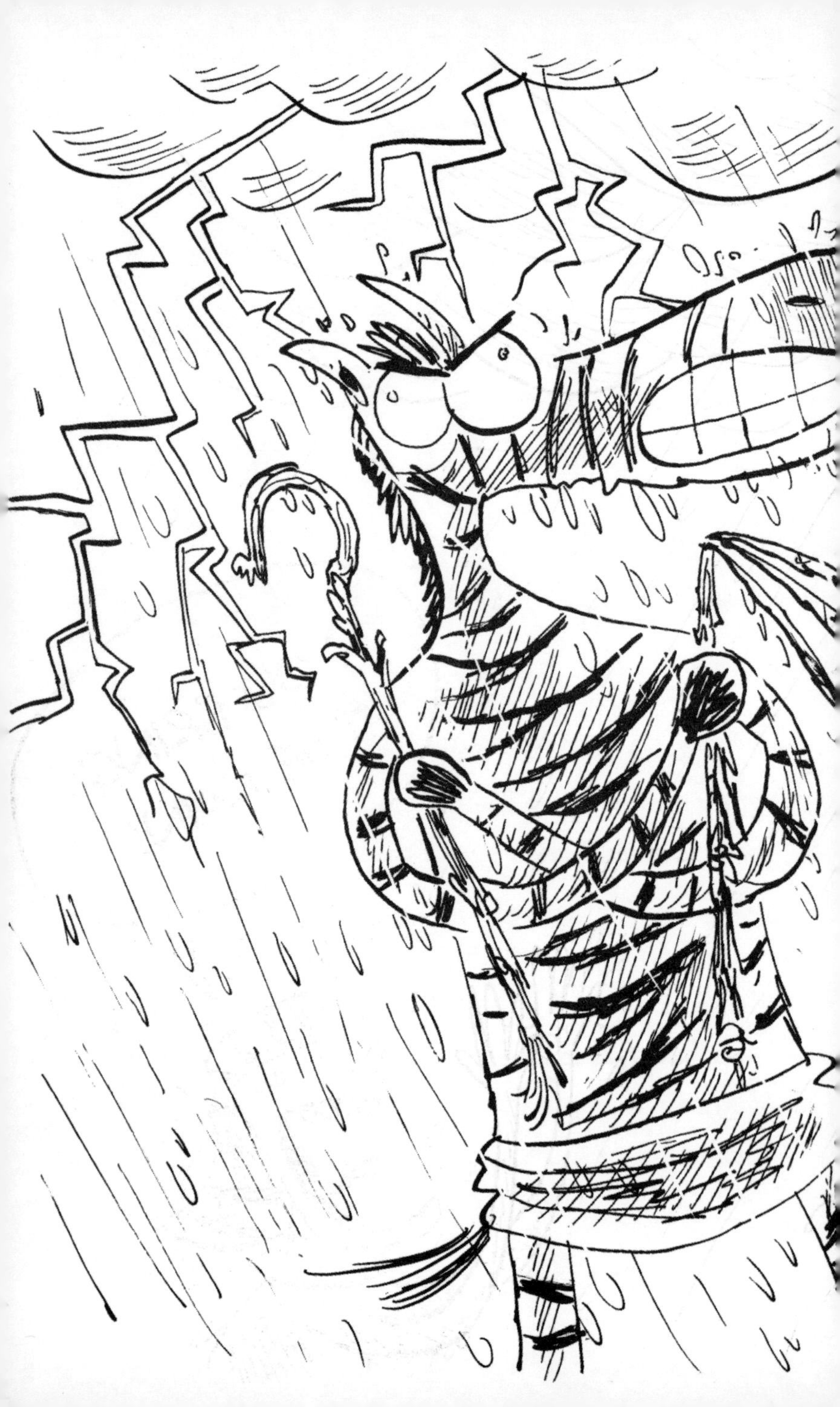

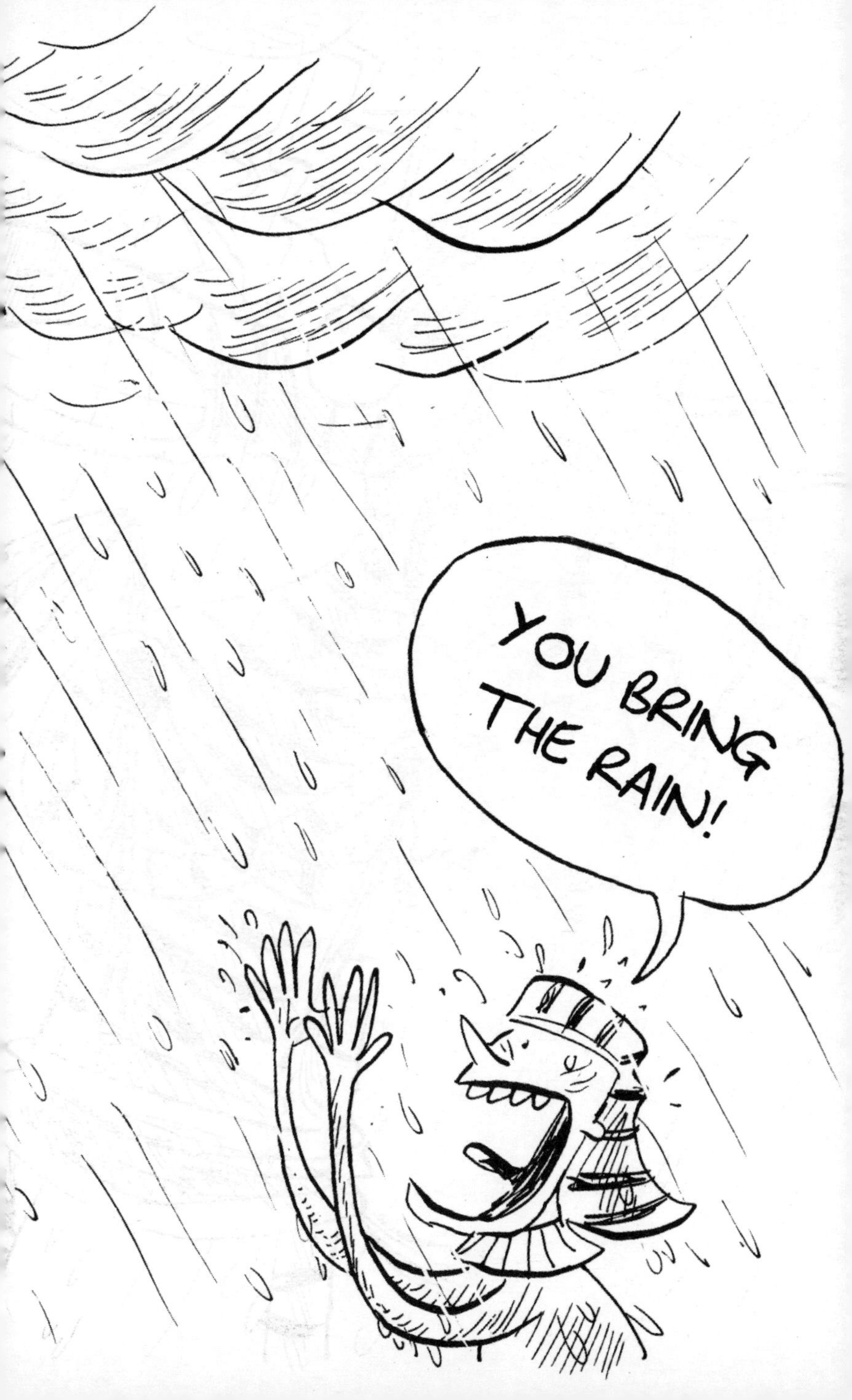
YOU BRING THE RAIN!

"Oh, he's good at that!" laughed Felix. "You should have seen him in Britannia. It rained everywhere he went!"

The soldiers threw themselves down at Julius's hooves. "Then it is as we suspected! You are the bringer of good fortune; you are THE CHOSEN ONE returned!"

"Now I've seen EVERYTHING!" Milus scoffed, laughing uncontrollably.

"But I don't understand," said Cornelius. "Why do you think HE is the Chosen One?"

"Because he brings the RAIN!" said one of the soldiers.

"But surely you must have had lots of rain during last night's storm?" Cornelius was very confused.

The soldier shook his head. "The storm at sea never reached our shores. Our crops are failing, but HETER has renewed our HOPE! He has answered our prayers!"

Julius was feeling even more perplexed. "HETER? Who's HETER?"

"Did ... did he just call me a horse?" Julius protested. "I'm nothing like a horse!"

The commander turned to one of his soldiers. "Make haste to Alexandria. Tell them to begin preparations!"

Tell them the Chosen One has arrived!

CHAPTER FOUR
HERO WORSHIP

"Come!" beckoned the commander. "We must hurry to our great city of Alexandria, where, as you are a returning god, our priests will surely proclaim you PHARAOH!"

Julius turned to Cornelius in disbelief. "But aren't pharaohs KINGS?"

Cornelius was just as bemused as Julius. "Well, they were last time I looked," he said. "You know, the

Egyptians do worship their animals and many ARE gods to them, as are the pharaohs!"

Little Pliny the mouse came running over. "What's all the big kerfuffle?" he asked.

They think I'm a GOD!

WHAT!?

"Not only THAT," interrupted Cornelius, "they want to make him PHARAOH!"

Pliny nearly fainted with shock. "I knew all that 'champion' gubbins would go to your head!" he squeaked.

"You know what?" Julius declared. "Maybe this is the BEST thing that could have happened to us!"

Cornelius looked sceptical. "What do you mean?!"

"Well, think about it," reasoned Julius. "For one thing, they don't want to kill us. Secondly, after all the nonsense we've been through, we deserve a bit of fun, a taste of luxury!"

Julius tapped the Egyptian commander on the shoulder. "Excuse me, will there be palaces and gold and stuff?"

"Of course!" replied the commander. "You will be ruler of Egypt; you can have whatever you want!"

Julius turned round to his chums. "See? We'll be living in palaces and EVERYTHING!"

We're finally going on our HOLIBOBS!

?

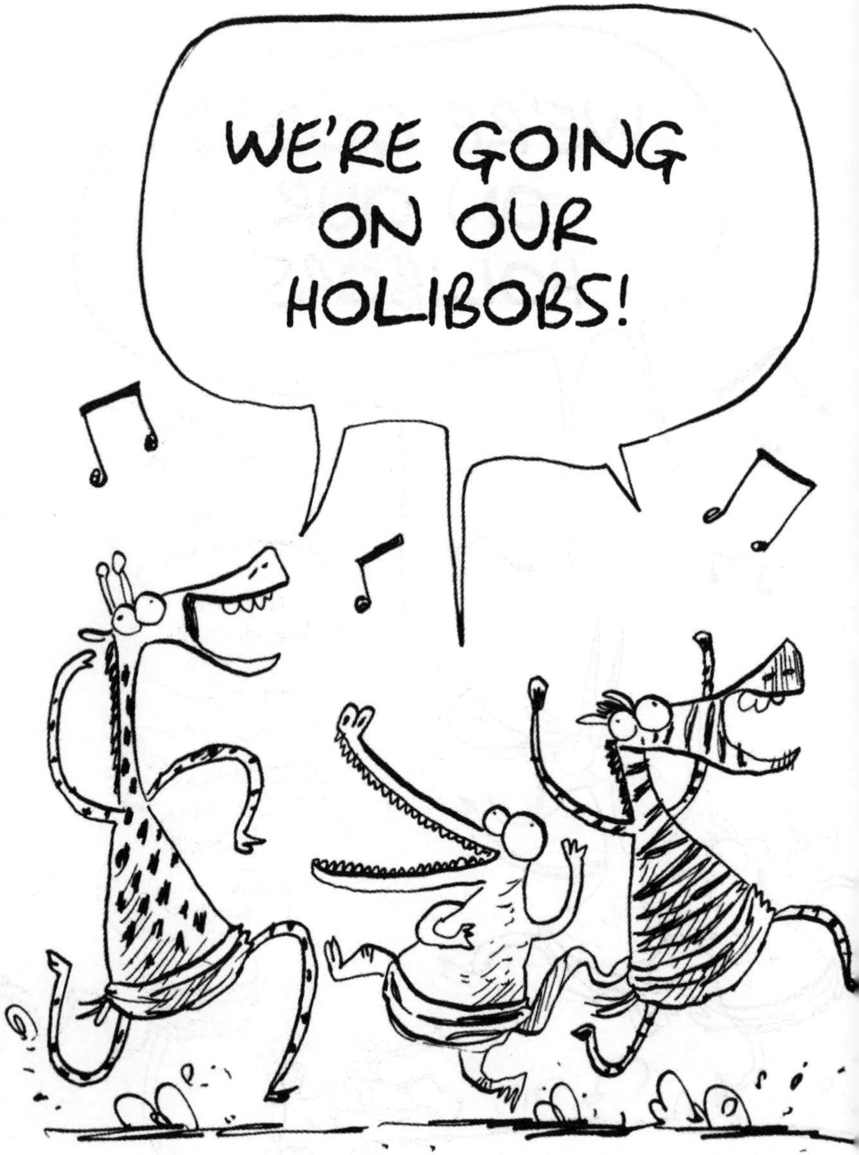
WE'RE GOING ON OUR HOLIBOBS!

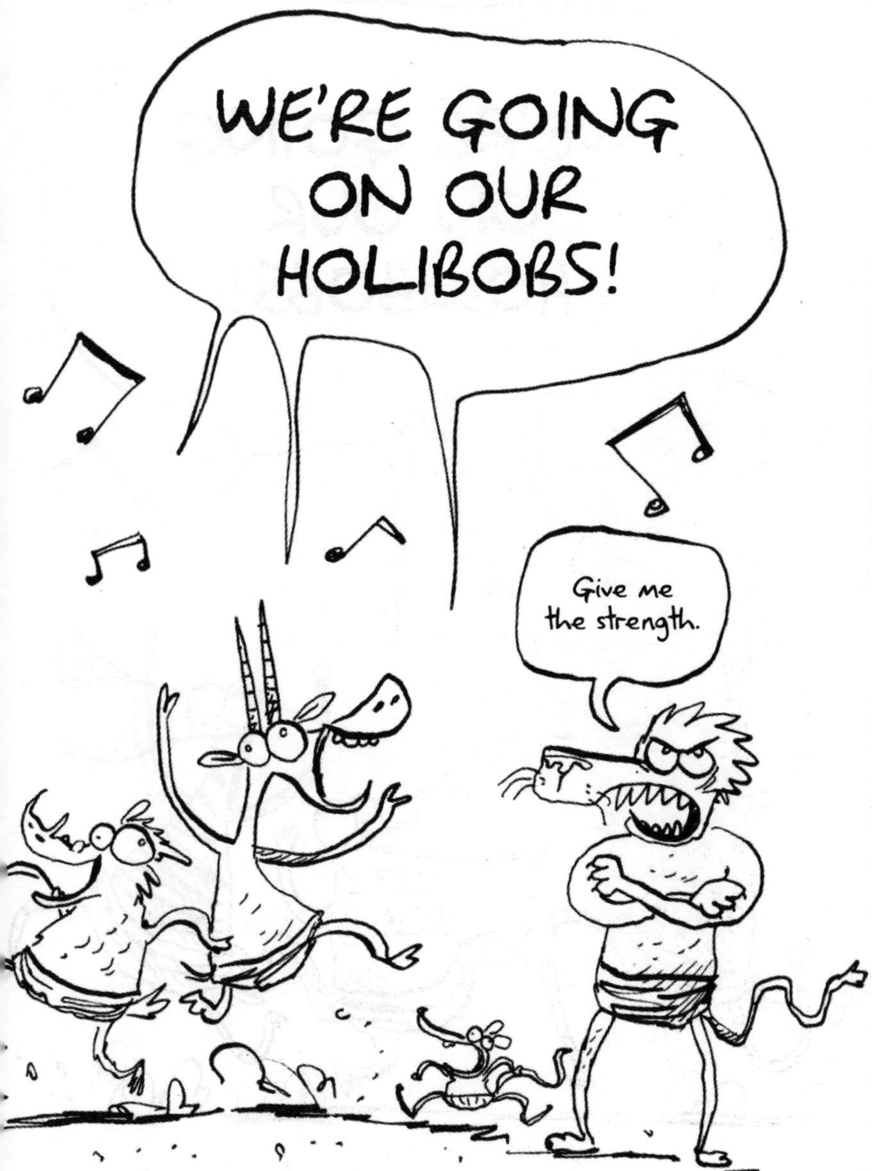
WE'RE GOING ON OUR HOLIBOBS!
Give me the strength.

Milus suddenly grabbed hold of Julius. "If you think ruling a country is going to be FUN, then you are in for a shock, donkey!"

Julius pushed the lion away. "You've always got to spoil things, you big grump."

"They also think you're a HORSE!" growled Milus.

When are you going to tell them you're a ZEBRA?

Before Julius had a chance to reply, the Egyptian commander gestured to them. "Come! We must be on our way," he ordered. "Word of your arrival has spread and the people of the Nile are overjoyed that you are here to save them and their crops!"

The commander was right. Along the road, farmers and fishermen had already gathered to witness the arrival of their new horse god.

Julius walked towards the eager crowd and began waving regally to them. "Stop worrying, Milus. Come on, let's have some fun for once!"

There was a sudden shrill cry of "OI!" from the beach. Everyone looked back to see what the fuss was.

"Everyone thinks Julius is a magic horse and they're going to make him king of Egypt!" replied Felix gleefully.

"They do?!" Brutus was very excited. "Cor! What a laugh!" He ran up to Julius and the soldiers. "Hey! I'm a magic horse too! Can I be a king? I've got a seaweed wig and everything!"

Julius and one of the soldiers turned round to face Brutus.

"Well?" asked Brutus indignantly, flicking his seaweed wig away from his eyes.

The soldier pulled the seaweed off Brutus's head and held it up disdainfully.

"Sorry!" said Julius apologetically, shrugging his shoulders. "It's out of my hooves. I'm sure you can still have fun with us in my palace, though!"

The soldier tossed the wig onto the ground and escorted Julius back to the road.

Brutus frantically scrambled after the seaweed, picked it up and dusted off all the sand. He looked up to see his brother disappearing into the distance. "Hey, wait!" he cried, plopping his wig back on.

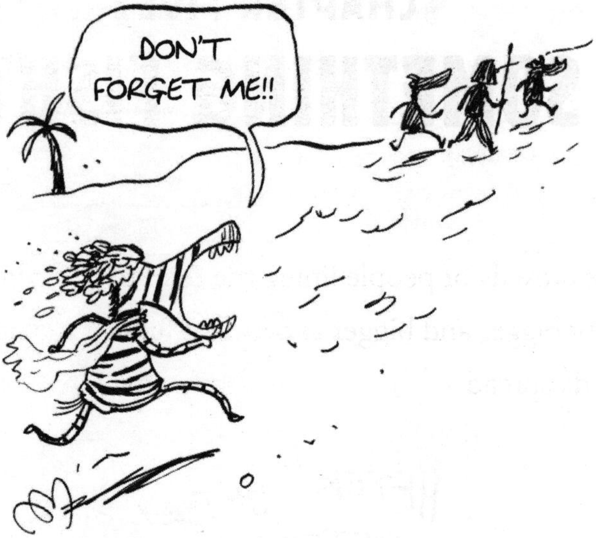
DON'T FORGET ME!!

❦ CHAPTER FIVE ❧
SOMETHING FISHY

The crowds of people lining the road to Alexandria grew bigger and bigger as word of Julius's magical deeds spread.

As Julius and his friends were led through a small fishing village, many well-wishers spilled out from the strange, square buildings. Julius could see young children, all sorts of traders and women carrying heavy pots on their heads. All of them seemed to be worshipping him!

Julius was really starting to enjoy the attention!

But Cornelius was becoming concerned. "Julius!" he whispered. "Maybe Milus is right. What will you do if they figure out you're not ACTUALLY a horse? They might kill you, or WORSE!"

"We'll have a bit of fun, fill our bellies with lovely food; then, when we've had enough, we'll run off one night when no one is looking."

As they made their way along the road, a small commotion erupted ahead, and the people began chanting "Heter!". There was a sudden great cheer, and cries of "Yippee!" and "Yahoo!".

"Wait a minute, what's happened?" cried Julius.

In the crowd, a little old man was hopping about with bountiful glee.

"Look! Someone seems very happy!" chuckled Felix.

I haven't worn this old loincloth since last summer. Yet when I put it on just now, I found a gold coin in the pocket!

The old man pointed at Julius. "And it's all because of HETER!"

Another great cheer went up and everybody started chanting Heter's name once again.

Felix and Rufus started clapping their hooves. "Oh, good work, Heter!" they said, deeply impressed.

"I'm really starting to believe in you!" laughed Felix, nudging Julius in the ribs. "You have AMAZING magical powers!" Then he leant closer and whispered in his ear.

In fact, I bet with your powers, you could easily find me a lovely Egyptian rock for my collection!

Julius pointed at a big stone right in front of them. "What are you talking about, you weirdo?" he scoffed. "There are rocks lying on the ground all OVER Egypt!"

OMIGOSH! THAT IS AMAZING!

Felix held up the drab, dusty brown rock as if it were a lost treasure. "BEHOLD! HETER HAS FOUND ME A BEAUTIFUL ROCK FOR MY COLLECTION!"

Everyone gasped at this miracle and once more began reciting the name of Heter.

Lucia started skipping along to the chanting crowd. "You're right, Julius, this really IS going to be fun!"

I can't remember the last time I felt this happy and free!

"Yeah, Julius," agreed Rufus. "Although I still haven't figured out how you made it rain; that was PRETTY weird!"

"My brother has ALWAYS been weird!" sniggered Brutus, joining in the skipping.

"Obviously I have hitherto unknown amazing powers!" chuckled Julius. "Who am I to question my godly abilities?" He wafted a hoof at Brutus. "Can you do something about that lump of seaweed on your head? It STINKS!"

You keep your mitts off my lovely wig!

Milus turned and snarled at Julius. "If you want to be a god, then carry on. Just let me go home!"

Pliny hopped onto Milus's shoulders and started giving them a good massage. "Come on, Mr Grumpy, if anyone needs this holiday, it's YOU!"

Julius put his arm round Milus. "Yeah, come on, grouchy. You can go home ANY TIME! Come and have a few days of fun with us!"

Milus gazed at all their smiling, encouraging faces and let out a big sigh. "Okaay..."

Pliny leapt off Milus's shoulders. "Wahey! I knew we'd twist your noggin!"

The commander beckoned the procession to continue. "We must march quickly if we are to reach Alexandria before sunset!" he urged impatiently. "Let us be on our way."

Julius clapped his hooves to attract everyone's attention. "Listen, everybody!" he yelled. "Today is probably the GREATEST day of my life!"

Julius cleared his throat and began to belt out an old favourite of his zebra herd. "SHE'LL BE ... COMING ROUND THE MOUNTAIN WHEN SHE COMES!" He waved his hooves, signalling everyone to join in.

"EXCELLENT!" cried Julius, and the procession trooped off towards Alexandria, merrily singing away.

CHAPTER SIX

A WARM WELCOME

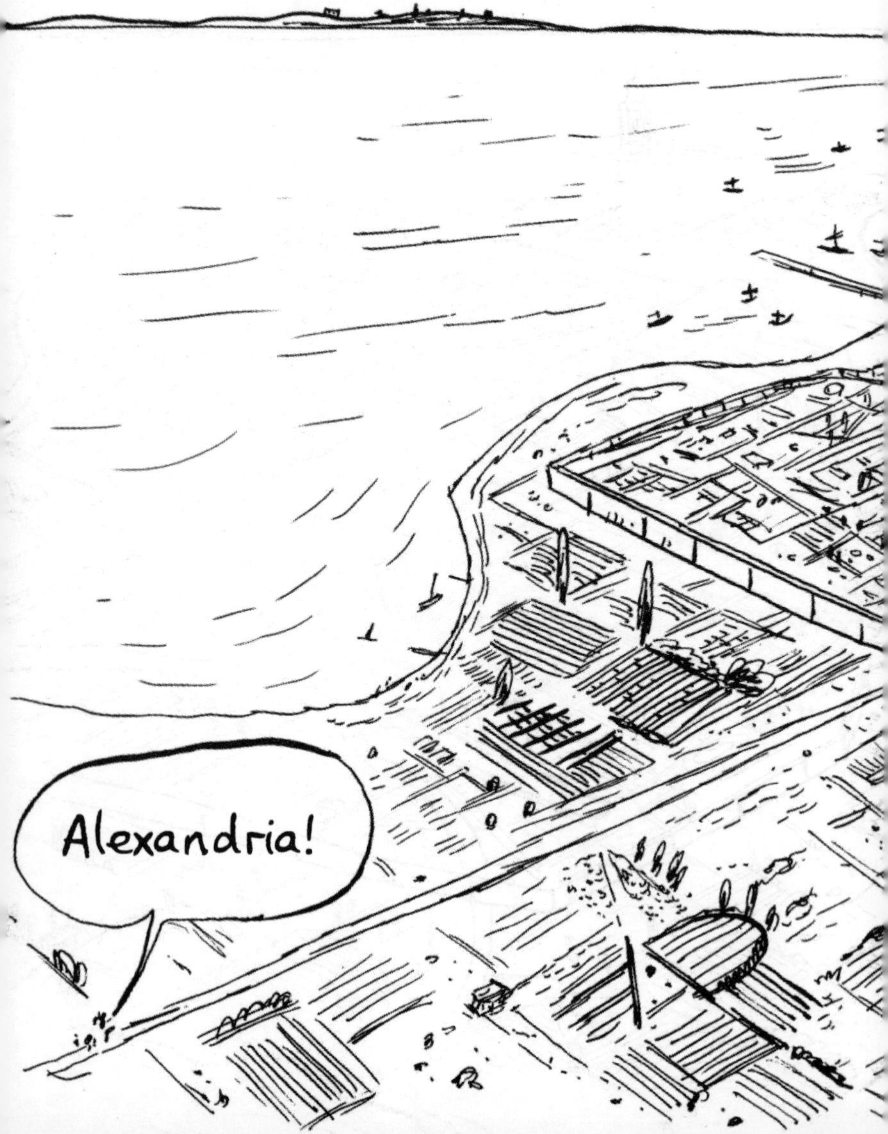
Alexandria!

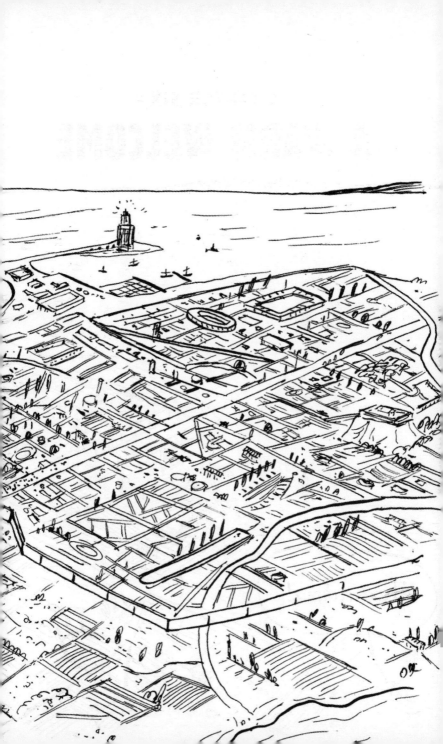

Wow, thought Julius, *this is a city to rival Rome itself!*

As they trekked past the tidy patchwork fields and smart temples and villas that lined the route to Alexandria, more and more people gathered to greet their new idol.

And as the great wooden doors to the city opened, Julius's eyes nearly popped out of his head at the sight of thousands cheering and crying out the name HETER!

The crowds parted to reveal a grand boulevard, hundreds of metres wide. Julius had never seen a road like it!

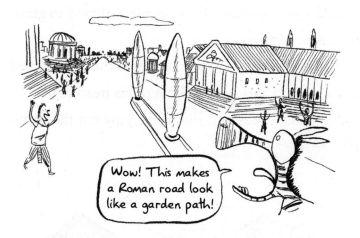

Wow! This makes a Roman road look like a garden path!

Julius boggled at the huge, gleaming temples and great statues lining the road as far as the eye could see. Giant columns painted with colourful figures were dotted everywhere.

What funny little people!

"Those are hieroglyphics!" said Cornelius helpfully. "The Egyptians use little pictures to tell stories instead of writing."

"Wow!" he marvelled, looking intently at the little carvings. "Hypergluesticks!"

Suddenly Julius spotted a MASSIVE tower in the harbour, just beyond the pillars and temples.

"That 'thing'," replied the commander proudly, "is our great lighthouse, Pharos. It is one of the Wonders of the World!"

Cornelius, not wanting to be left out from sharing interesting facts, butted in. "Yes," he agreed, "it uses a mirror to reflect the sun's rays during the day and a fire is lit on top during the night."

"Well, you know," said Cornelius modestly, "I've read the odd parchment."

The commander laughed. "The odd parchment, you say? Then, my little friend, you are going to LOVE our library!"

"It is true," said the commander. "Julius Caesar himself tried to destroy it many years ago." He halted the procession and threw his arm out to the left.

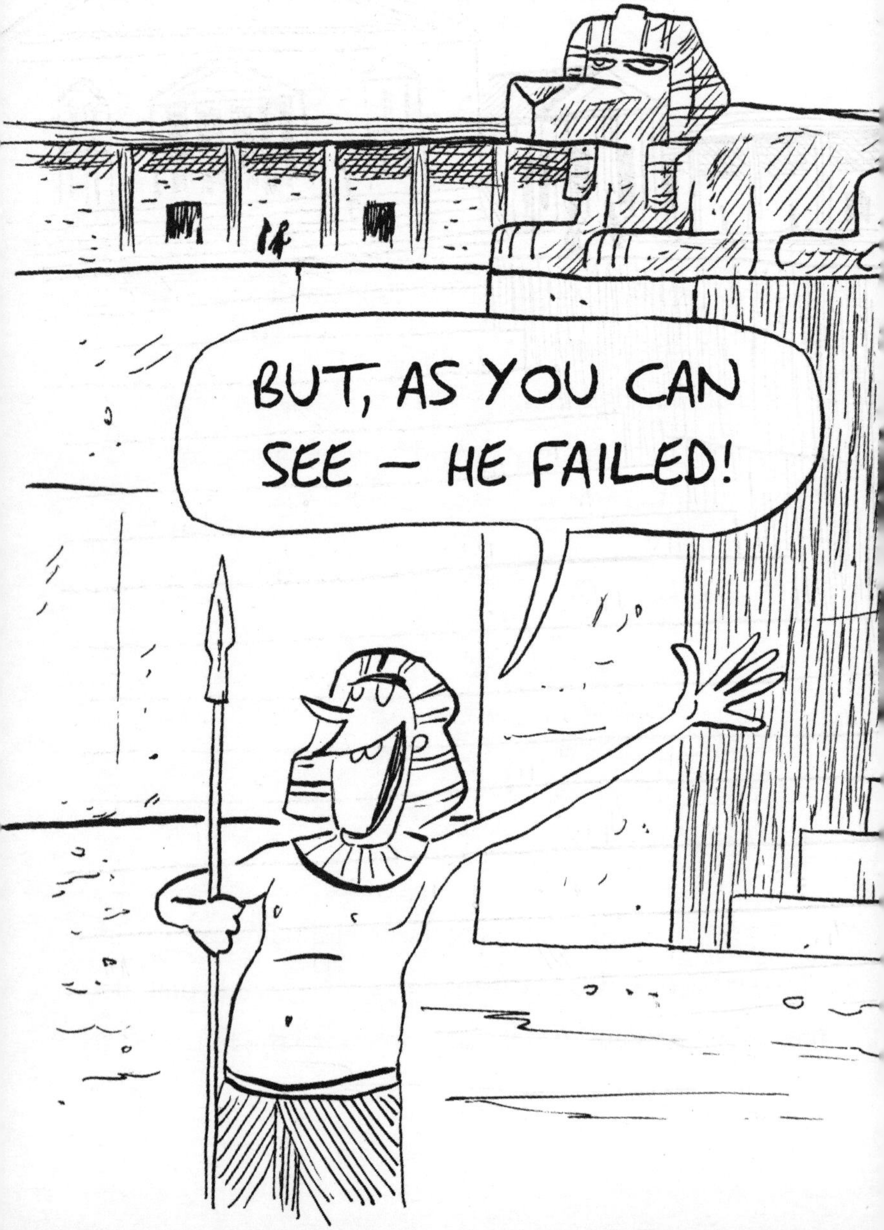
BUT, AS YOU CAN SEE – HE FAILED!

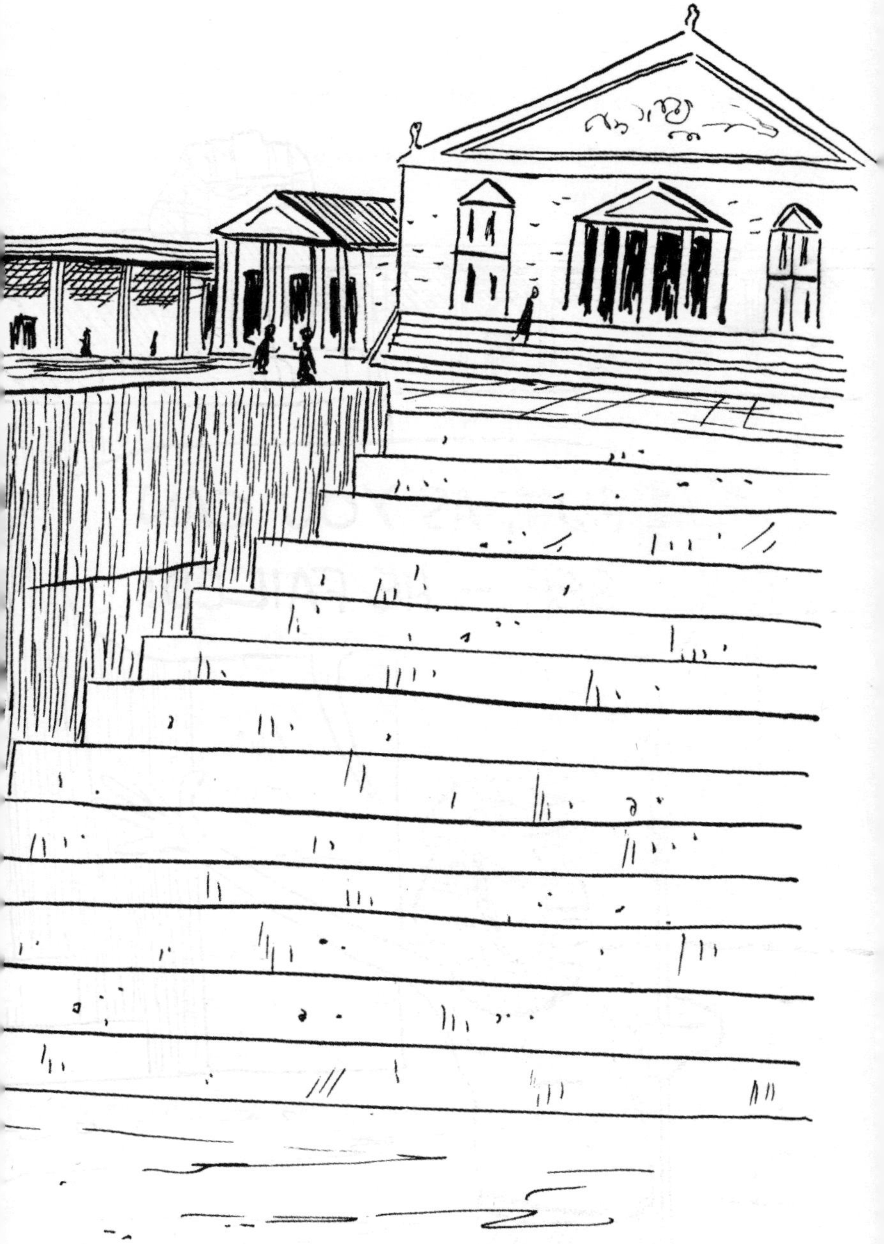

Julius was feeling a bit lost. "What are you guys even talking about? First a lighthouse, now a libra-HAIRY!"

Cornelius was hopping about with glee. "A library, Julius, a LIBRARY! The greatest library the world has ever KNOWN!" He laughed. "Centuries of knowledge and wisdom from all over the world, stored here for everybody to read on scrolls and parchments."

Whatever you want to know, ANYTHING, you will find it in HERE!

Julius looked intrigued. "What, even about zebras and grass and stuff?"

Cornelius grinned from ear to ear. "Yes! Even about zebras and grass!"

Felix sauntered over and put his hooves on his hips. "So, are you telling me," mused the intrigued antelope, "that in there somewhere, there's a scroll about all the rocks that have ever existed on earth?"

Cornelius laughed again. "EVERY ROCK, ON HUNDREDS OF SCROLLS!"

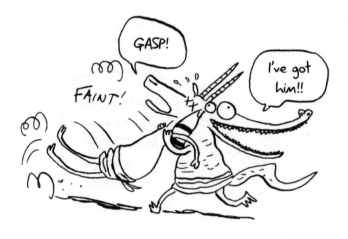

"But first we must meet with the priests," said the commander. "Then, when your friend is crowned pharaoh, you can visit the library whenever you please!"

The procession turned off the great avenue and continued along a road, much more narrow, though no less grand. Mighty statues of fantastic-looking beasts lined the street, alongside excited well-wishers all hoping to catch a glimpse of their new god.

The commander laughed. "Those are your fellow gods. It would be unwise, perhaps, to mock them!" He suddenly thrust up his hand and the procession came to an abrupt halt.

"Hey, why have we stopped?" asked Julius.

"Because we are here!" exclaimed the commander.

"Where's 'here'?"

"Let's hope he's not watching TOO carefully," growled Milus under his breath.

‹ CHAPTER SEVEN ›
THE ORACLE

Julius could just make out the figure of a small bald man wearing a plaited white skirt standing at the top of the steps to the temple. The sun glinted off the man's head as he beckoned the zebra towards him.

"Wait, aren't you all coming with me?" asked Julius nervously.

The commander shook his head. "Only priests and gods can enter the temple."

"Oh, right," gulped Julius as he anxiously began to climb the steps. "Just me, then…"

Cornelius scampered after his friend. "Hold up, I'm not letting you go on your own!" he cried.

"WAIT!" shouted the commander. "ONLY GODS ALLOWED!"

Felix turned and shouted back, "BUT WE'RE ANIMALS! YOU EGYPTIANS WORSHIP US, RIGHT?"

And with that, they all dashed up the steps after Cornelius and Julius, leaving the commander behind.

"Watch him, Julius!" warned Cornelius. "He'll try to pretend HE is the horse god!"

"We can't have that idiot ruling Egypt! Quick!" And Julius sprinted after his brother.

Brutus raced off far ahead. "You can't catch me!" he laughed, skipping nimbly up the last few steps.

Julius took a deep breath, snorted through his nostrils and, with an extra burst of energy, flew up the rest of the marble stairs.

"You stop right there, you rascal!" bellowed Julius, leaping into the air and tackling Brutus.

"Oi! WATCH IT!" screamed Brutus as he slammed to the floor. "I was only messing about!"

Julius immediately leapt to his hooves and saluted the priest. "Heter, god of instant rain and magic coins, at your service!"

The priest was not impressed.

Brutus pulled himself up too and adjusted his very smelly seaweed wig, then grabbed the priest's hand and shook it vigorously. "And I'm Brutus, brother of Julius, I mean HETER!"

"Get your filthy hoof OFF me, you stinking BEAST!"

Brutus glanced at Julius, confused. "'Ere, I thought you said they liked animals?"

Cornelius and the others finally caught up with Julius and Brutus at the top of the steps. "Going well, then, is it?" puffed an out-of-breath Cornelius.

"Oh, brilliantly," replied Julius with a sigh.

There has obviously been a mistake. You buffoons do not fit the description of any gods that I know of!

Cornelius nudged Julius hard in the ribs. "Quick! Give him that speech you gave those soldiers on the beach this morning!"

Julius stood puzzled for a moment, then suddenly realized what Cornelius was on about.

"Oh, yeah!" he said. "That proper did the trick, didn't it!" He stood in dramatic fashion. "Now, what was it I said? I'm not sure I remember." He gave a little cough to clear his throat.

I AM JULIUS ZEBRA, ENSLAVER OF THE CHAMPIONS, DESERTER OF ROME AND, ER, ... SAVIOUR OF THE BISCUITS!

Julius rubbed his chin, thinking hard. "No, wait," he said, waving his hoof at the priest. "That doesn't sound right. Well, it was something like that, anyway!" He chuckled.

"There will be NO crown for you, cretin!" cried the priest. "Nor do we look kindly upon those who seek fame and fortune by grasping the crown FALSELY for themselves!"

"Didn't I tell you?" muttered Milus.

All of a sudden a voice called out from the courtyard behind them. "Stand aside, Imhotep," the voice wheezed. "Let the creature through!"

The priest was caught off guard. "But, Your Holiness, there is no way this fool—"

The priest reluctantly stepped aside and waved Julius on. "Please," he hissed, "the Oracle in his infinite wisdom wishes to speak to you."

Julius turned to his friends and shrugged. As he made his way through the pillars, Cornelius and the others began to follow him, but the priest thrust his staff in front of them. "Not you lot," he said firmly.

Julius entered a large courtyard alone. To the left stood an imposing temple, very similar to all the Roman ones he'd seen on his travels, with its triangular roof and multiple columns.

As Julius drew closer to the temple, the butterflies in his stomach whirled around. He didn't much like the sound of the icy, creepy voice that came from inside and had to stop himself from running away.

"Do not be afraid, young zebra," said the voice.

Julius was shocked. "But how do you know I'm a ZEBRA?"

Through the gloom, Julius could see a small figure in the shadows.

"When word reached me of a brash horse claiming to be the 'Champion of Rome' and 'Liberator of

Enslaved Beasts', well," the voice chuckled, "there could only be one creature in the entire Roman Empire fitting THAT description!"

"Come closer, young gladiator." The shadowy figure beckoned to Julius to step inside the temple. "I am an Oracle. I see things that no other man or beast sees."

Julius stepped gingerly into the darkness. "Do you have magic eyes, or something?" he asked.

The figure laughed. "Yes, something like that." He shuffled over to Julius and gazed up at him. "I come from a long line of Oracles. We see into the future and we see into the past."

"How about round corners?"

The shadowy figure ignored him. "My great-great-great-great-grandfather once met a soldier called Alexander in the desert many miles from here, many, many years ago. He saw in him a GREAT man, a man who could unite the warring tribes and empires. This was the very same man who went on to conquer Egypt and numerous other countries, and whose children and grandchildren ruled our lands for hundreds of years."

The man pulled out a piece of parchment from his cloak and held it up to Julius.

This is it! thought Julius. *The Oracle has foreseen my coming and I'm to be PHARAOH OF EGYPT!*

The Oracle coughed nervously. "Young zebra, would you make an old man happy and let me have your autograph?"

"If it's not too much trouble." He strolled over to a pile of papers on a desk behind him. "I have quite a collection, you know." He held up an old parchment. "Look, here's Cleopatra's signature! Isn't it beautiful?" He shuffled through some more papers. "This is Theseus, the Greek who defeated the Minotaur. Such a nice chap."

"But I thought you were going to see whether I was worthy of being a god and a pharaoh? Not ask for autographs!"

The figure ambled back over to Julius. "Oh, goodness, yes, by all means, be our pharaoh. You can't do much worse than the rotters who run the place at the moment!" He held out his parchment again.

CHAPTER EIGHT
ROMANS OUT!

Julius emerged from the temple to a great roar from the crowd. The priest stopped him and looked him up and down. "Well, what did the Oracle say?"

Julius pushed him to one side and addressed the crowd.

The Oracle has spoken: I AM YOUR NEW PHARAOH!

As the onlookers once again roared their approval, Cornelius went up to Julius. "Gosh! Well done, Julius!

That's AMAZING! You must have really impressed him. Oracles are very wise old men."

"Nice work, Julius!" exclaimed Felix. "But where's your crown?"

"Good point!" Julius turned to the priest. "Have you got my crown then, please?"

The priest, still unimpressed with Julius's earlier shenanigans, could barely bring himself to look at the zebra. "Patience, *Your Highness*," he growled. "There will be a coronation for you in three days' time. Arrangements will be made for the ceremony at the old city of Memphis, in the shadow of the great pyramids."

Cornelius could barely contain his excitement. "Did you say THE PYRAMIDS?! WOW! This trip just gets better and better!"

Julius was none the wiser. "What's so exciting about a pair of mitts? Chilly Romans wear them all the time in Gaul!"

The pyramids, Julius! The Great Pyramid is one of the Wonders of the World!

"Cor, they do like their wonders out here," said Julius.

"But these are the wonders of ALL wonders!" cried Cornelius. "Huge mountainous triangular tombs that practically touch the sky, so they say." He folded his arms smugly. "To this day, scholars still don't know how they built them. Each stone block weighs a ton!"

"Ooh, I must get one for my rock collection!" enthused Felix. "Imagine one of those on my mantelpiece!"

Suddenly a short fat man in a smart toga came puffing and panting up the steps.

"I suggest you take care," warned the priest. "Here comes Titus Flavius, the prefect. He is the man in charge from Rome!"

Julius was baffled. "Rome? What have they got to do with the price of eggs?"

"Egypt is a Roman province, Julius!" replied Cornelius. "They OWN Egypt!"

"They're not rioting!" protested Julius. "They're cheering for me! I'm the Chosen One. The new PHARAOH!"

Flavius nearly exploded with rage. "PHARAOH?!" he squealed, his face red like a big tomato. "Have you lost your SENSES? Our Great Imperator, HADRIAN, is ruler of these lands. No other!"

"Try telling it to THAT lot!" said Julius, pointing to the crowd.

HETER! HETER! HETER!

The Roman prefect recoiled in shock. "But this ... this is MADNESS!" He stared at Julius. "Who are you that DARES come here to claim the throne?"

"I am HETER, the horse god, bringer of magic rain and coins," declared Julius proudly. "Although you might also know me as Julius Zebra, Champion of the Colosseum!"

Flavius gasped in surprise and leant forward, squinting at Julius. "It cannot be...?" Rotten fruit splattered against the prefect's lovely clean toga. "HEATHENS!" he yelled, waving angrily at the crowd, which roared angrily back. Fearing their wrath, Flavius scurried off towards the temple. Once safely on the threshold, Flavius turned and risked a final shout at the onlookers below.

And with that, he was gone.

"He's not going to get very far in that temple," observed Julius. "Isn't that the only entrance?"

"No," replied the priest. "There are many

secret tunnels and corridors throughout this city. Flavius will easily find his way out."

Julius clapped his hooves. "Does this mean I'm free to rule Egypt, then?"

"I would say so," replied the priest. "But we should be prepared for a visit from Hadrian and his army. Now that word is out about your arrival, he won't be a stranger to our shores."

"Oh, don't worry about him," laughed Julius. "I easily kicked his butt back in Britannia!" He turned to the priest, who was standing nearby, arms crossed, staring grumpily at the zebra. "And you and me, we're all square, right?"

Perhaps, beast, perhaps not.

We shall see.

The priest sloped off back to the temple.

"What did THAT mean?" worried Julius.

"I warned you, Julius," said Milus. "There will be those in Egypt who won't be happy that you've just strolled up and taken the crown."

The lion started walking back down the steps. "Have your fun for a few days, then let's leave this crazy place, before it's too late."

Julius just tutted and shook his head. "Some people are no fun AT ALL!"

CHAPTER NINE

BATH TIME!

Julius lazily splashed the milk in his bath as he took another swig of grape juice.

From the other side of the room, Felix let out a satisfying groan. A big Egyptian, built like an elephant, was massaging the antelope's shoulders as he lay flat on a marble slab.

Julius laughed. "Soon you'll feel like a new antelope!" He dunked his head under the milk, then rose out of his bath. The waiting handservant quickly threw a towel around the dripping zebra. "And how about you, Milus?" he called out. "Are you still in a rush to head back home?"

Cornelius trotted into the room looking quite sprightly. He chuckled at the lion. "Don't be so dismissive of donkeys, Milus!"

"Why?" Milus said, narrowing his eyes. "What's it to you?"

"Well!" the little warthog said, grinning, "that milk you're sitting in is DONKEY'S milk!"

WHAT!?

Cornelius tottered over to Julius, who was sniffing his wet arms. "You know," he said, "I was told Cleopatra swore by this stuff. Makes your skin look young and beautiful, apparently!"

Julius rubbed his chin thoughtfully. "I wonder if I can get zebra milk imported?"

"Most likely," replied Cornelius. "You, Lord Heter, can have whatever your heart desires, from what I can gather."

Julius turned to a little Egyptian sitting patiently next to the bath. "SCRIBE!"

The little man jumped to attention.

"Make a note that I would like to import zebra milk," demanded Julius regally.

"Yes, my gracious lord," said the scribe, hurriedly scratching away on his parchment.

With that, the little man left the room.

Cornelius sidled closer to Julius and glanced around to see if anybody was listening. "Julius, I've been thinking about what Milus has been saying and I'm worried about some of those things the priest said yesterday." He looked around again. "If they find out you're not who they think you are, you might be in grave danger," he whispered.

"Bah! You worry too much, Cornelius!" scoffed Julius. "Why do you need to go to the library?"

"I want to read more about this prophecy of the Chosen One!" replied an anxious Cornelius.

"What are you two whispering about?" asked Felix.

"Cornelius wants to go to the library to double-check the prophecy!" Julius told him quite loudly.

Lucia swanned in, flanked by Rufus, Brutus and Pliny. "Ooh! Did someone say something about libraries?" she asked.

"GOOD GRIEF!!!" exclaimed Julius, his eyes nearly popping out. "What on EARTH are you lot WEARING?!"

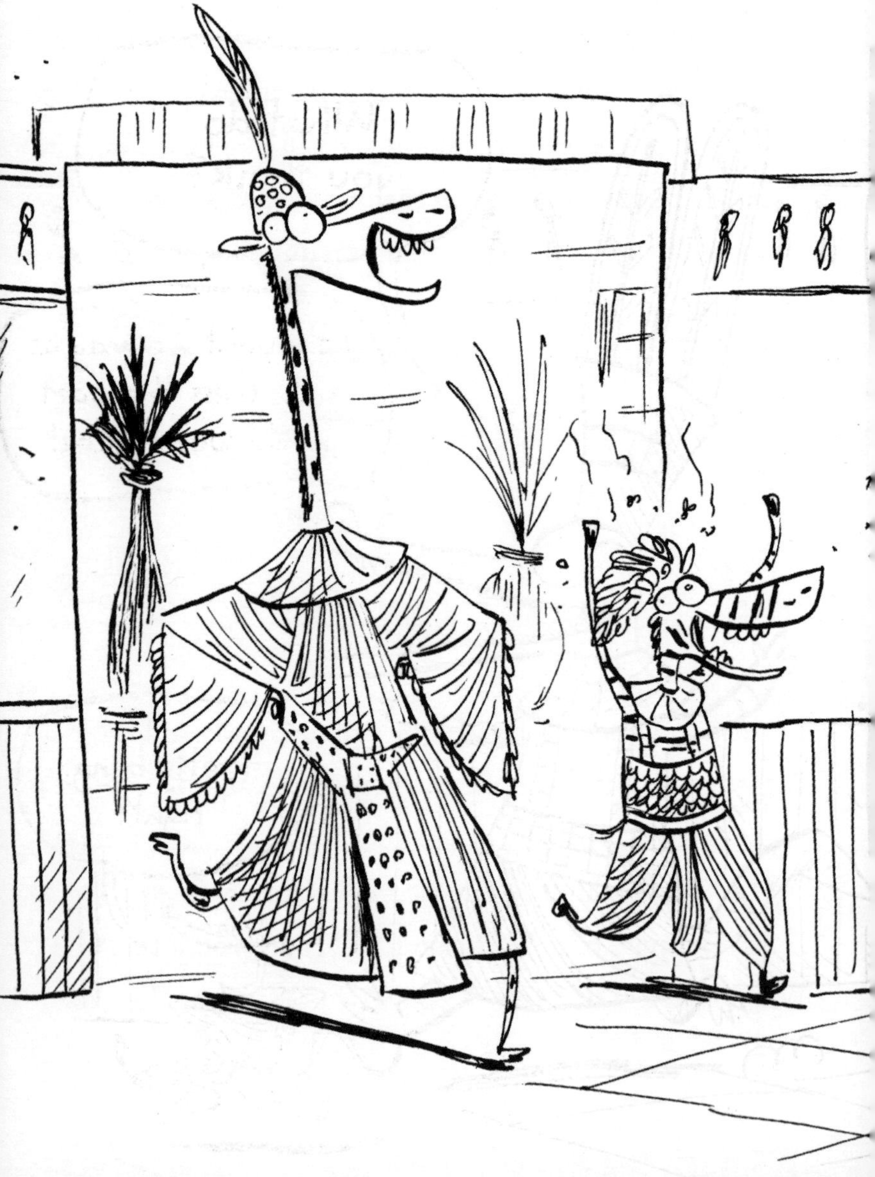

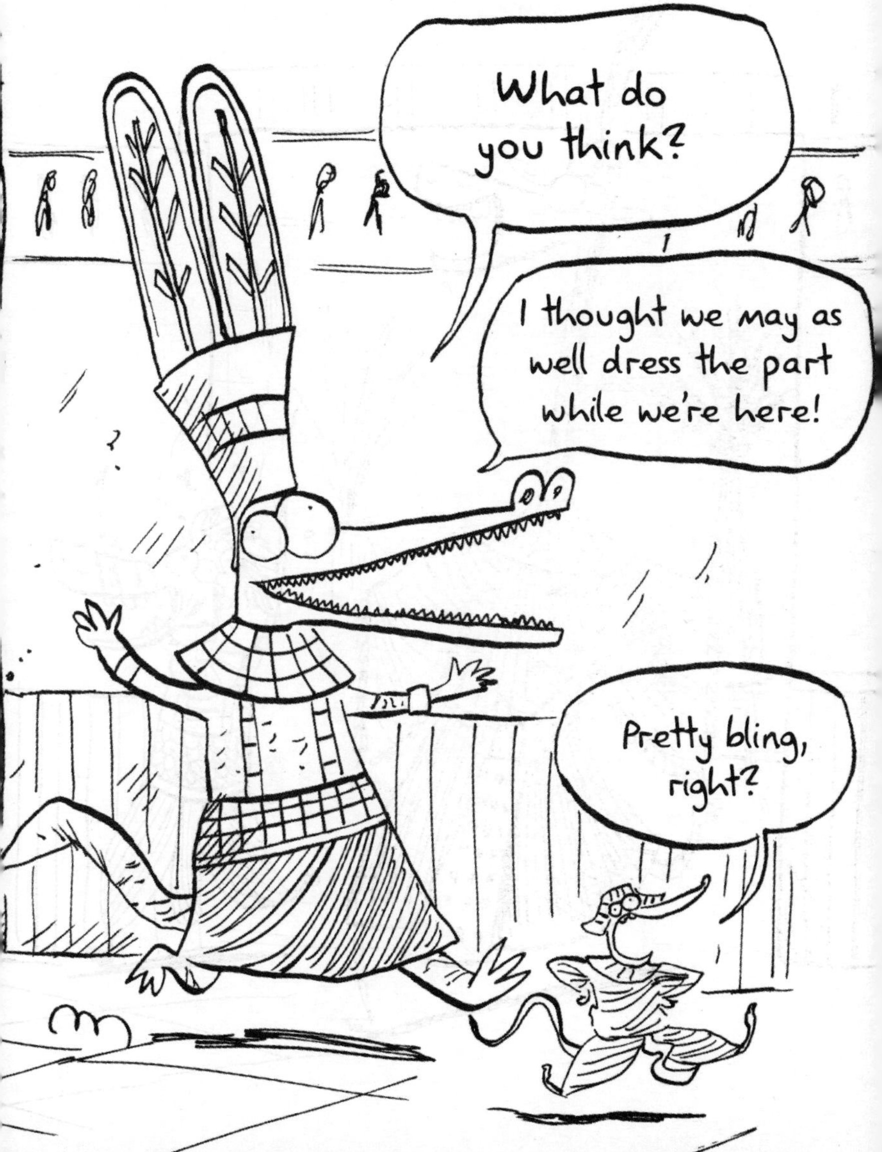
What do you think?
I thought we may as well dress the part while we're here!
Pretty bling, right?

"I want me some of these crazy clothes," declared Julius. "I am the new pharaoh after all!"

"Me too!" exclaimed Felix. "Where did you find them?"

"In the Royal Wardrobe," said Lucia. "I'm sure we can rustle up a lovely skirt and headdress for you, Felix!"

Cornelius was at the end of his tether. "Chaps, seriously!" he huffed. "We need to visit the library now, before it closes at sunset!"

"All right!" tutted Julius. "Don't get your tusks in a twist."

CHAPTER TEN
BURNING QUESTIONS

"Wait for me!" cried Julius as he tottered up the marble steps uneasily. "It's flippin' hard getting around in this tight skirt!"

As well as his ill-fitting clothes, Julius also had to deal with the eager crowds desperate to touch their new pharaoh.

Brutus decided to jump in and help his poor brother. He roughly pushed the onlookers to one side. "Keep back!" he ordered. "I, Brutus, brother of the Chosen One, command you to keep back!"

A young Egyptian boy was impressed. "Ooh, are you Heter's brother?"

"That's right," replied Brutus, trying to look regal. "We're completely related to each other."

"Then you TOO must be a god!"

Brutus nodded in agreement. "You'd think so, wouldn't you? Try telling that to the PRIEST though!"

Julius grabbed Brutus and dragged him away. "Oi! Stop all that!" muttered Julius. "Why don't you just let it drop. It's becoming ever so slightly annoying now!"

Well, it's not fair! How come you get to be a god?

I'm just as brilliant as you!

"Perhaps when you make it rain out of nowhere, or summon coins from the sky," said Julius, "then we might have a second look at your magical credentials."

Brutus stood at the bottom of the stairs, fuming, as Julius and the others carried on towards the library's entrance.

"WELL, MAYBE I CAN!" he cried out. "WATCH THIS!"

Julius turned round to see Brutus with his arms in the air, his face scrunched up in desperate concentration.

"What IS he doing?" wondered Felix.

Julius shrugged. "Trying to make it rain, I think."

Brutus's face was starting to go scarlet as he willed with all his might for it to rain. "I can feel it coming!" he gasped. "I DEFINITELY have magic powers too!"

The Egyptians burst into laughter at poor Brutus.

"Why's everyone laughing?" he cried. "At least I got one raindrop!"

"Keep it up!" sniggered Julius. "You might get a downpour if you're lucky!"

With that, Julius hitched up his skirt and they all scooted up the remaining steps into the gleaming white marble courtyard.

At last they reached the entrance to the library, which was guarded by grim-looking statues of lions wearing stripy Egyptian headpieces.

Look at those grumpy lions! They must be relatives of yours, Milus!

"Come on!" urged Julius as he sprinted into the library. "Cornelius ran on ahead. He must already be inside!"

Milus plopped himself under a lion statue. "You lot carry on. I'm staying right here."

Grrr.

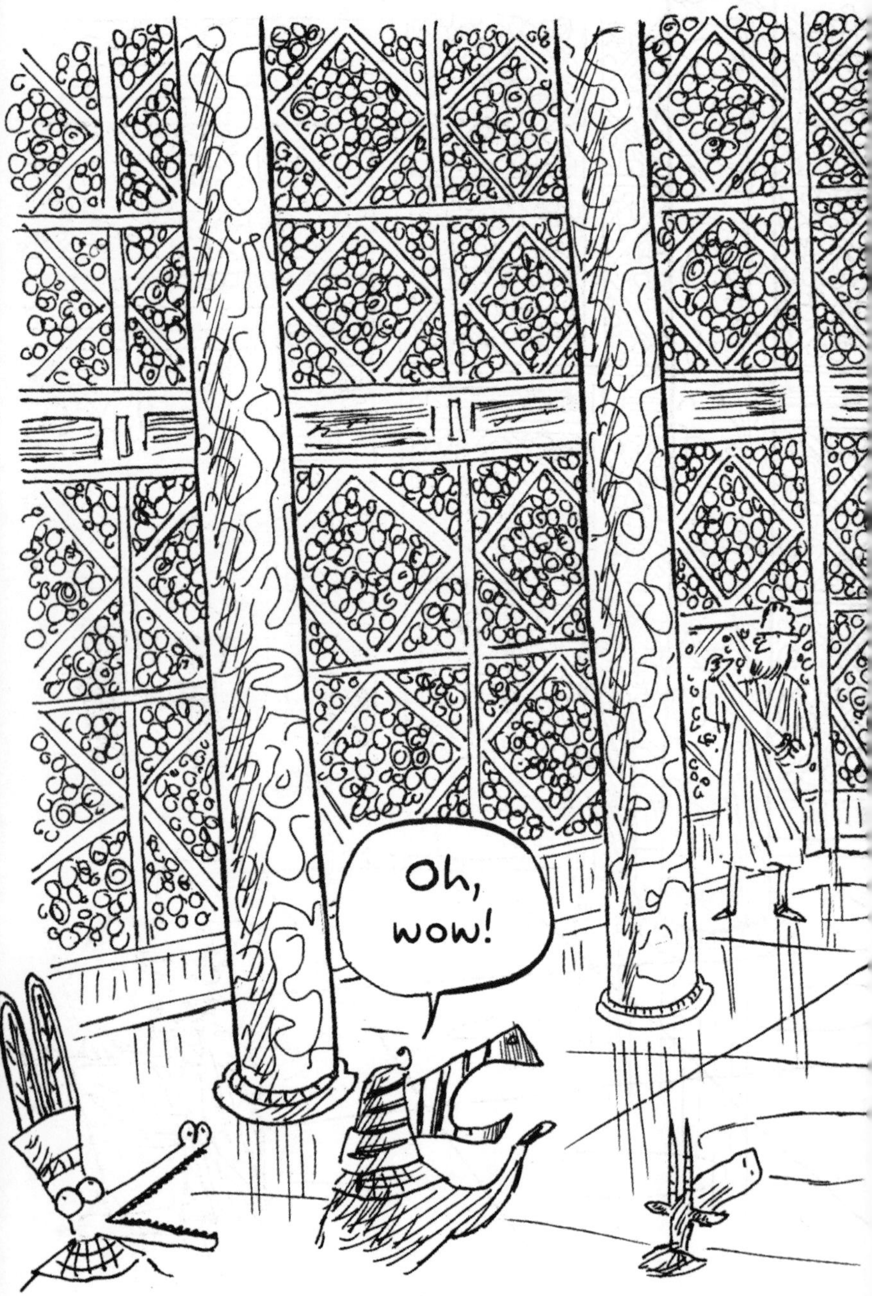
Oh, wow!

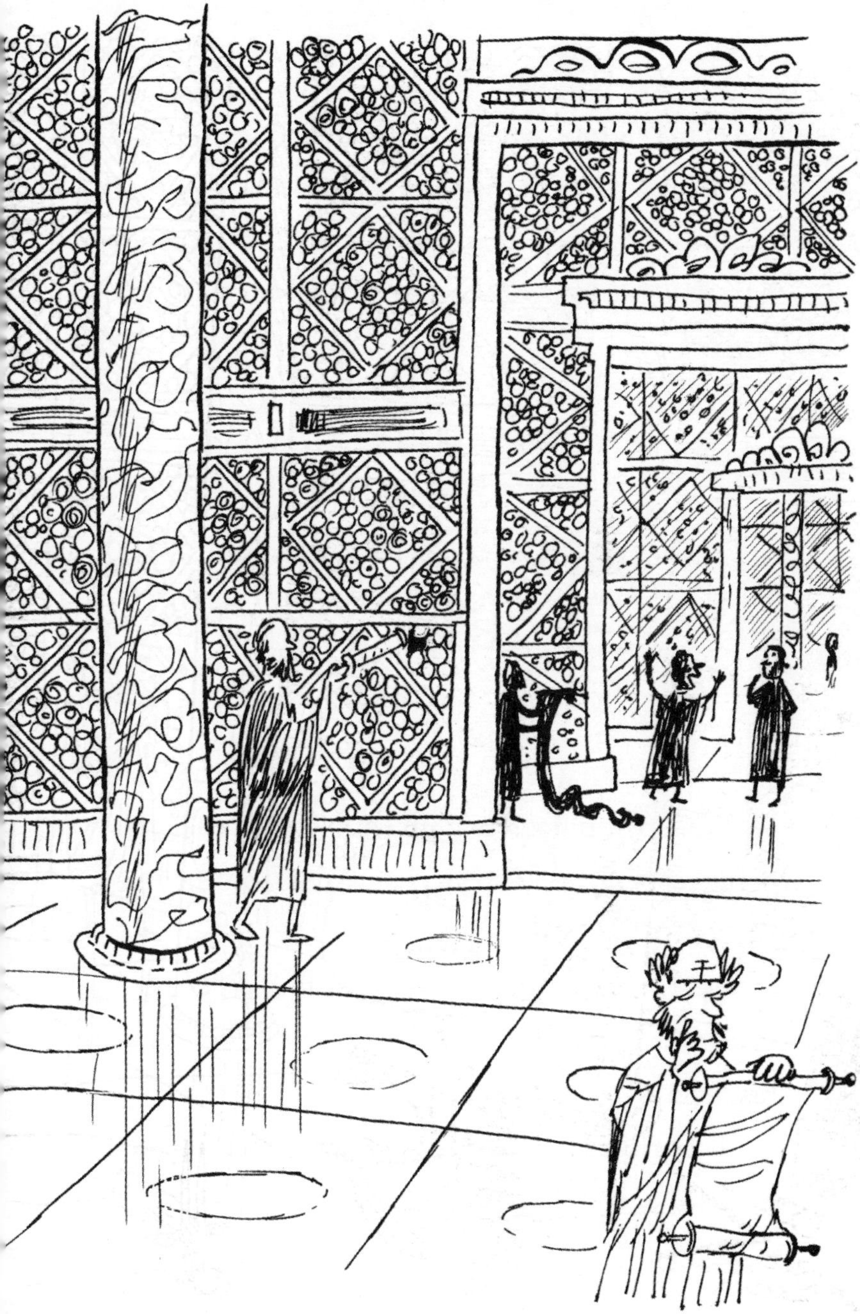

"That warthog could be anywhere!" cried Julius. "Come on, let's ask the chap at the desk."

Julius sauntered up to the desk and gave a polite little cough to attract the attention of the busy librarian.

"Well, first point," said Julius, slightly put out at not being recognized. "I'm your new pharaoh, so you'll address me as 'Your Majesty'."

The librarian sighed indignantly and rolled his eyes. "Yes, what is it ... *Your Majesty*?" He inclined his head.

"THAT'S BETTER!" laughed Julius and held up his hoof for a high five.

Julius's hoof hung awkwardly for a few seconds, before he realized the gesture wasn't going to be reciprocated. He lowered his hoof and gave a second, more nervous, cough. "Um," he stammered, "you, er … didn't happen to see a little warthog come in, did you?"

The librarian's left eyebrow arched upwards. "If you are referring to *Phacochoerus africanus*, then yes, he proceeded through the doorway to the west." He pointed to the door behind Julius.

Lucia grabbed Julius by the arm and dragged him away. "It's the posh name for warthog!" she hissed.

"It IS?" blurted Julius. "How do you know?"

"Let's just say Cornelius has referred to himself by that name on more than one occasion," she replied.

"Well, our Cornelius does like posh words," nodded Julius.

They walked through the tall doorway to find a room filled from floor to ceiling with scrolls. Each wall was crammed with neatly stacked V-shaped shelves that were marked by subject matter. At the far end, among a group of browsing scholars, was Cornelius, surrounded by many scrolls scattered on the floor.

"What does it say?" asked Julius excitedly. "Am I in there?"

Cornelius turned round and scrunched the scroll up very quickly. "SHH!" he said, putting his little hoof to his lips. "No, Julius, you are not in here. Well, not exactly."

Julius read the scroll carefully, making murmuring noises as he did. "Interesting, *verrry* interesting," he muttered, tapping his chin thoughtfully.

Cornelius snatched the scroll back. "You're reading it upside down, you idiot!"

"Yeah, I know!" protested Julius. "We pharaohs can read in ALL sorts of directions!"

"CAN you now?" huffed Cornelius.

"Oh, stop being a grump! Just tell us what it says."

What are all these ones?

They look very old!

"All these scrolls are about the history of the Egyptian people and, in particular, prophecies," explained Cornelius.

He unrolled the scroll Julius had pretended to read and pointed to a small passage. "See here, it talks about the return of a Chosen One to save the Egyptian people from hardship and to restore the country to its former glory."

Cornelius nodded. "Yes, you have. Well, *Heter* has, to be precise."

Cornelius grabbed Julius's arm and dragged him back down. "Hush, you two! Try not to make a scene."

The other scholars were tutting and shaking their heads.

The little warthog continued. "That is only part of it—"

But before Cornelius could finish, Felix dashed over clutching an armful of scrolls.

"Check it out!" he cried, and threw the scrolls at his friends.

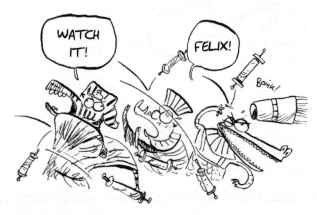

"I must protest!" spluttered Cornelius. "These scrolls are IMPORTANT artefacts and must be treated with GREAT CARE!"

"That's EXACTLY what the librarian said," reflected Felix. "You should get a job here, Cornelius!" The antelope unravelled one of the scrolls. "This place is amazing, look!"

Suddenly Brutus, Pliny and Rufus appeared clutching their own scrolls.

"Wotcha, lads!" said Pliny. "How's all yer learning going?" The little mouse brandished his scroll. "These drawings show fighting techniques from around the empire. I'm proper learning these!"

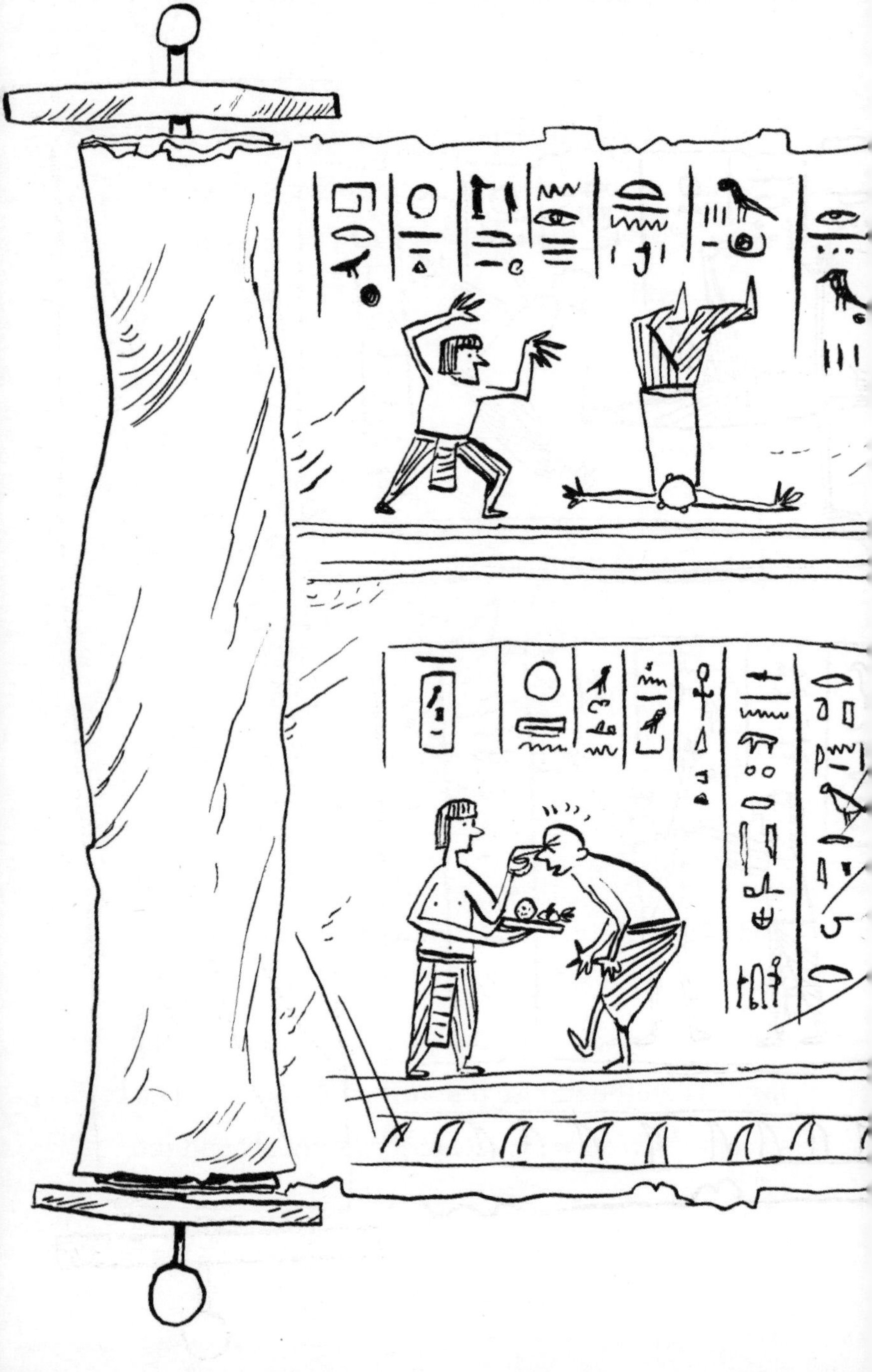

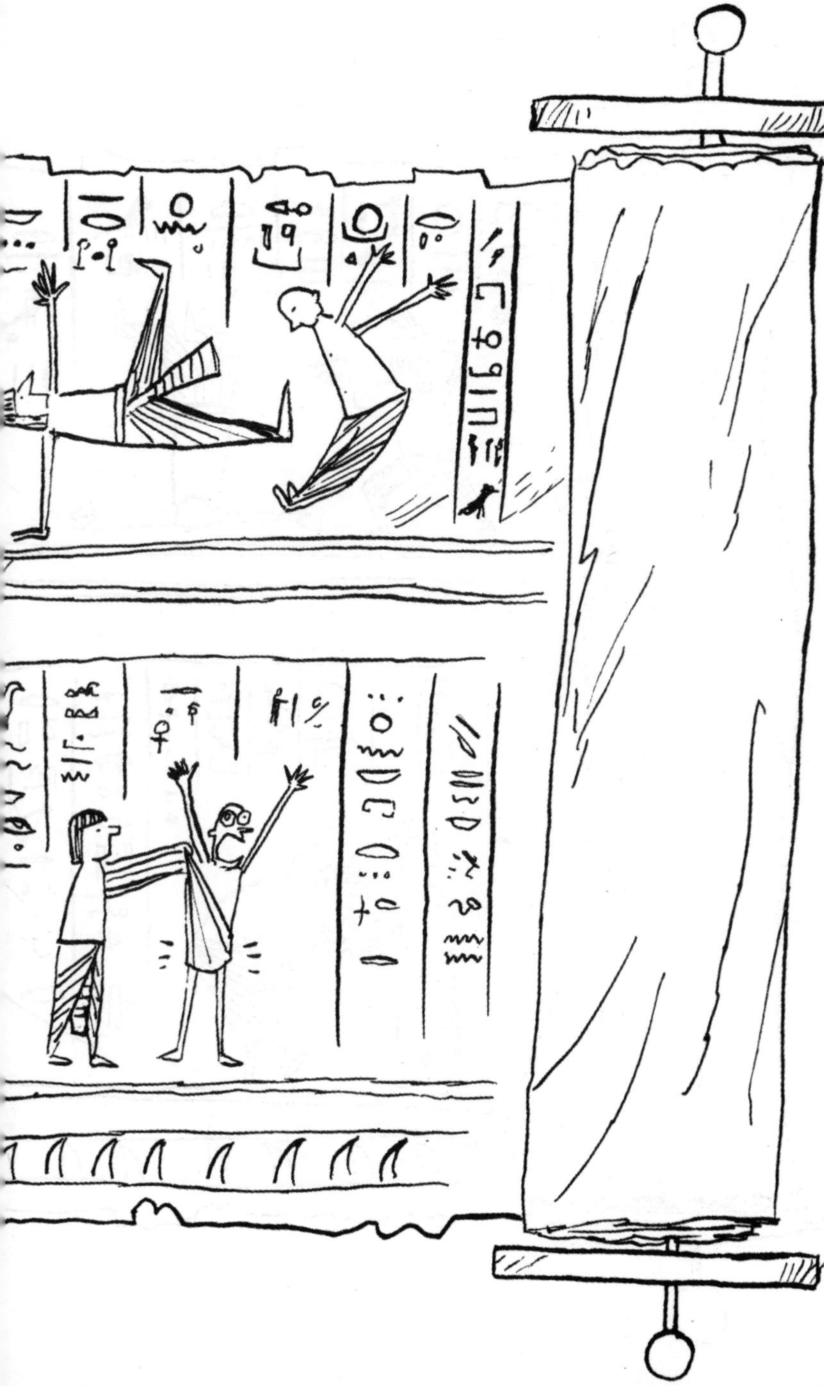

"I've already got one of the moves worked out!" squeaked Pliny. "Watch THIS!" He grabbed Felix by the ankles and tossed him through the air like a caber.

That's an Hispanic Ankle Throw, apparently!

SMASH!

Very useful.

Rufus also showed off his scroll excitedly. "I found one which has all the rules for my board game! Did you know it's called Ludus? We might actually know what we're doing now!"

"And you, Brutus?" asked Julius, raising his eyebrows and expecting the worst.

"Come again?" blurted Julius.

"Gastromancy," announced Brutus, reading aloud the words on his parchment, "is the ancient Greek art of conversing with the voices who speak to us via our stomachs."

"He's lost the plot!" said Lucia.

"No, hear me out," protested Brutus. "You know all that bleeping and blooping that goes on in your stomach? It's ACTUALLY your belly trying to talk to you!" He tapped his scroll. "According to this, the voices can even predict the future."

"Never mind all THAT!" shouted Julius, before realizing all the scholars were frowning at him. He motioned for everyone to huddle closer. "Cornelius was about to tell me something important," he whispered. "Weren't you, Cornelius?"

Cornelius unravelled his scroll again solemnly. "Yes, I was, Julius. But I'm afraid it's not good news."

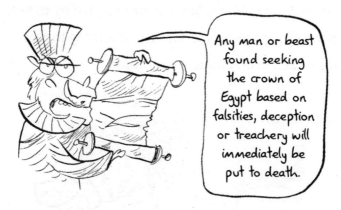

Any man or beast found seeking the crown of Egypt based on falsities, deception or treachery will immediately be put to death.

Julius gave a big gulp and sat down heavily.

Felix patted Julius on the shoulder. "Oh, hard luck, Julius. It's been nice knowing you."

Cornelius held up his hoof. "But that's not all."

THAT'S NOT ALL?!

IT DOESN'T GET MORE FINAL THAN DEATH!!

Cornelius hushed Julius then carried on reading from the scroll. "Any collaborators, conspirators or parties found colluding with the accused shall also be put to death."

"WHAT?!" screamed Felix. "But isn't that US?!"

"I'm afraid so," replied Cornelius, rolling up the scroll firmly.

CHAPTER ELEVEN
FRIENDS IN HIGH PLACES

As they hurried back to the palace, they were greeted by Imhotep the priest.

"Your Majesty," said the priest impatiently, before bowing dramatically to Julius. "We were just about to send a search party. Your presence is urgently needed!"

The flustered zebra tried to squeeze past Imhotep. "Can it not wait?" he blustered nervously. "I, er ... have my own urgent business!"

We are to leave immediately for Memphis!

"But I thought the coronation was tomorrow?" said Julius.

"It IS," replied Imhotep. "But we must set off now to begin preparations."

Julius gulped in despair and dashed up the stairs to his room. "We'll be back down in a minute!" he called out.

"Fear not!" said Cornelius confidently. "We'll escape through those hidden tunnels and catacombs the priest was talking about. The palace must be rife with them!"

The animals ran into the pharaoh's main chamber and Julius set them all to work immediately. "Right, this is the plan!" he announced. "I want everyone to check each nook and cranny for a SECRET TUNNEL!"

Oh, I DO love a puzzle!

"This isn't fun and games," snapped Julius. "This is LIFE OR DEATH!" He clapped his hooves. "Quickly, before baldy-locks gets back!"

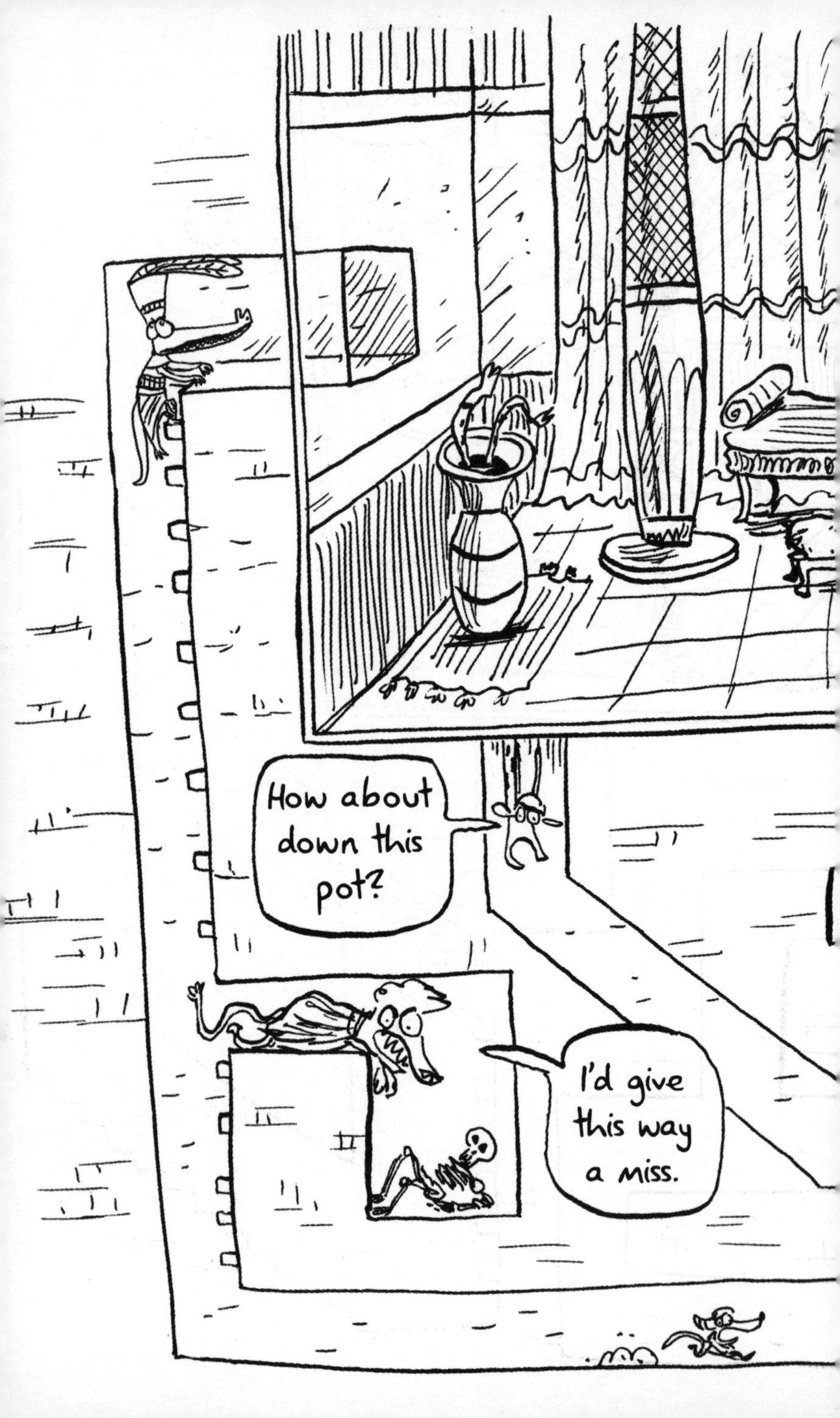
How about down this pot?
I'd give this way a miss.

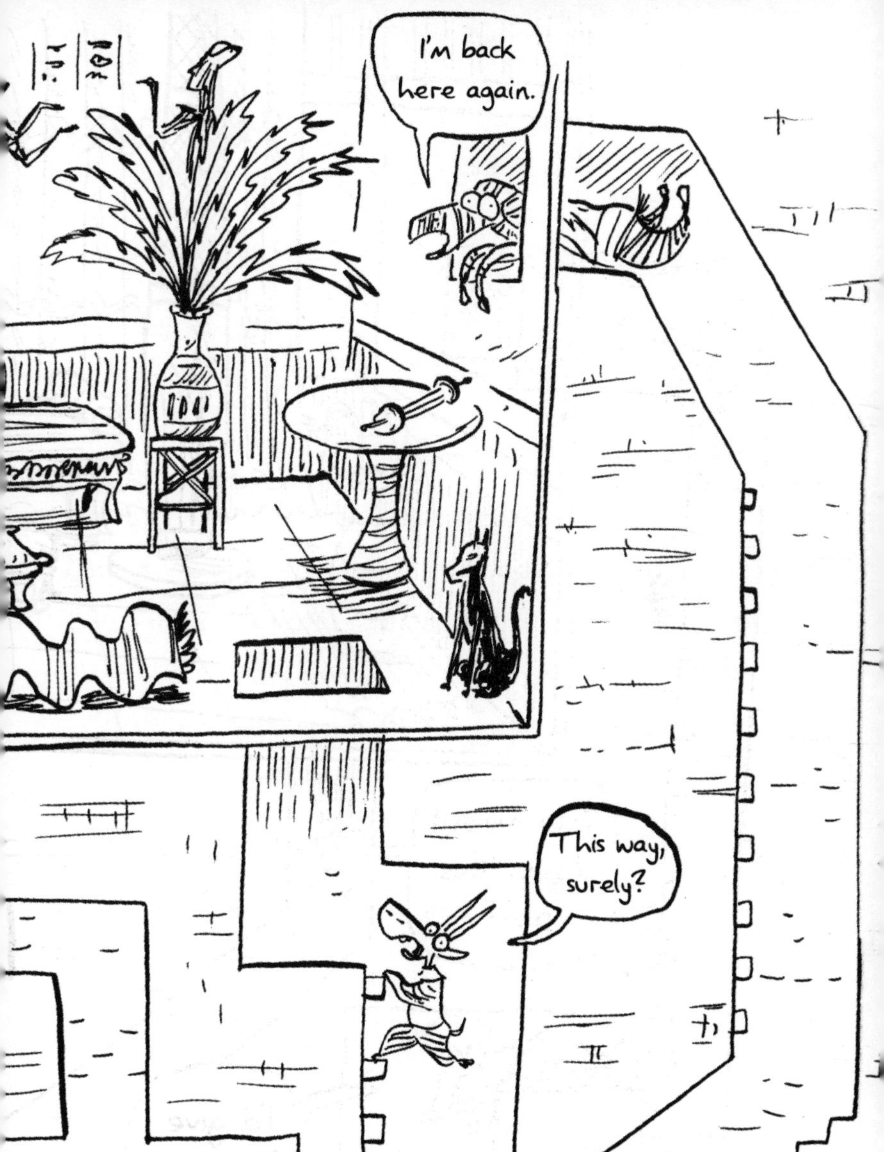
I'm back here again.
This way, surely?

The sound of hard sandals galloping up the marble stairs caught everyone's attention and Julius swivelled just in time to see Imhotep burst into the room.

"Rats!" muttered Julius. "We're too late!"

"Your Majesty," sneered the priest. "We can wait NO LONGER. We must leave immediately, before the sun sets."

As they were herded down the stairs, Julius whispered in Cornelius's ear, "We'll just have to go along with it and hope for the best!"

Cornelius nodded. "It doesn't look like we have much choice."

Outside, they were met by an impressive entourage.

"This way to the jetty, Your Majesty." The priest beckoned to the steps leading down to the harbour.

Cor! It's SO golden!

As Julius stood on the jetty, he was overwhelmed by a sweet fragrance. He stuck his nose in the air and took a deep breath. "Whew! What an AMAZING smell of flowers! Check it out, everyone!"

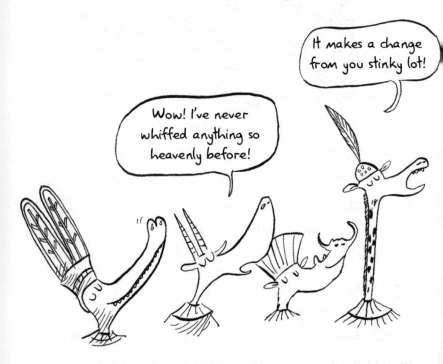

Waiting to greet them on the barge was a very smart and very smiley Egyptian. He clapped approvingly at everyone's royal garments.

The Egyptian held out his hand to clasp Julius's hoof and bowed. "It is a great honour to meet you, Lord Heter," he said. "My name is Apepi and I am the captain of today's flotilla."

"Very nice to meet you, Apoopi," said Julius graciously.

"*Apepi*, Your Majesty."

"Of course," replied Julius. "That's what I said. And may I say what a lovely-smelling boat you have."

Apepi bowed again. "My pleasure, Your Majesty. My family and I are eternally grateful for the rain that you brought to save our harvest."

Apepi showed Julius to his seat. "Your Royal Majesty may sit here under this silk canopy, if it pleases you."

"Ooh, very snug!" said Julius, plumping himself among the big cushions.

"And your friends," continued the captain, "can sit under the poop."

Cornelius pulled Brutus under the small golden canopy at the back. "It's not THAT sort of poop, you fool!" he chided. "It's just another word for the roof of a cabin!"

All the other animals made their way to the small cabin and tried their best to find a place to sit.

"Shove up!" said Pliny. "There's room for all of us!"

Brutus still had the grumps. "How come we have to squash in, while old pharaoh-face gets to sit on those big cushions up front?"

"Yeah, please don't wind up Pliny," warned Felix, "or he's liable to chuck one of us into some bookshelves."

Rufus nudged up to Brutus and pulled out his old board game and a pouch of stones. "Come on, let's have a game of Ludus to take your mind off it all."

Brutus reluctantly joined in a game, but he still wasn't happy. "I've been talking to my stomach and it totally agrees that I should be pharaoh too."

You'll be swimming with the crocodiles and talking to their stomachs if you don't shut your beak.

The barges finally set off from the jetty and Apepi called over to Julius. "Would Your Majesty like some music for the journey?"

Julius clapped his hooves together excitedly. "Ooh, YES PLEASE!" he squealed. He leant over to his friends at the stern. "Right, you lot, stop squabbling. I want to hear this!"

From one of the barges at the front, a small group of musicians began playing a soft melodic tune.

"Oh, I like this!" Julius grinned.

Forgetting all his troubles, Julius sank back into his soft cushions and soaked up the view as they left the harbour of Alexandria.

After a short distance the flotilla turned into the mouth of the Nile. Julius waved at all the crocodiles floating idly in the river. "Cooee!" he called out.

Julius waved regally at the various people and animals on the riverbank they passed. *You know, I could get used to this pharaoh malarkey,* he thought.

But, as the day wore on, Julius began to feel rather hot under the blazing sun.

"Take your headdress off!" suggested Cornelius. "No point in overheating."

"Yeah," agreed Julius. "Good plan, Cornelius. My head is getting proper sticky."

He reached up and removed his headpiece. A small but welcome breeze blew across his forehead.

But no sooner had he exposed his head, than a voice called out from a small crowd on the riverbank. "Cooee! Julius! Hello! It's me!"

Julius sat up with a shot. "Did someone just call out my NAME?!" he gasped, diving for cover behind his silk cushions.

"I can't believe it!" cried Julius. "Who knows me out HERE?!" He slowly peeked through the crack of two cushions. "Omigosh," he exclaimed, closing the gap shut. "Isn't that Annie the gnu from the lake back home?"

"What, that weird one who's always yapping to Mum?" asked Brutus, straining to see who it was.

"Yeah, that's the one!" said Julius. "I'd recognize that beard anywhere. What's she doing all the way up here in EGYPT?!"

Everyone lay flat on the deck until the barge was well and truly far away from the gnu.

When they thought they were far enough away, Julius finally flopped back onto his cushions.

"Let's just hope old Imhotep didn't see or hear her!" replied Cornelius ominously.

The barge sailed down the Nile for a few, less eventful, hours. Julius carefully waved to all the happy well-wishers in their boats lined up along the riverbank, careful to keep a beady eye out for any more familiar faces. But, thankfully, he didn't see anyone else he knew. Julius was in fact quite struck by just how pleased everyone was to see him. *What will they do when they find out who I really am?* he thought.

As the sun started to set and a cool breeze floated across the river, Apepi came over and bowed to Julius. "Good news, Lord Heter!"

Julius sat up and rubbed his tired eyes. The captain pointed to the horizon, where three triangular silhouettes seemed to rise up from the Nile.

Julius sprang to his feet. "CORNELIUS, LOOK!" he yelled. "You were right!"

Cornelius woke from a slumber. "Wait ... I was? What about?"

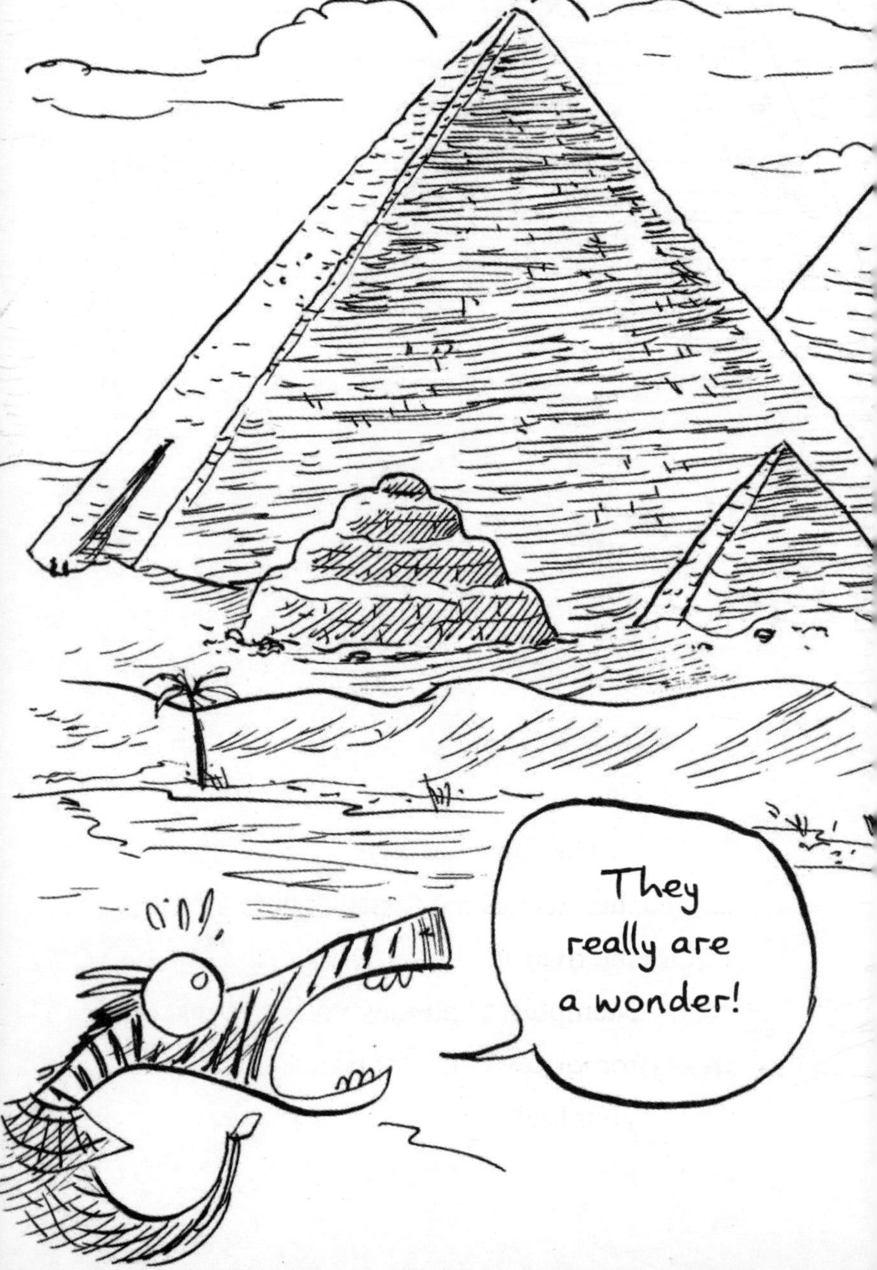
They really are a wonder!

The captain ushered them all to
their feet as the flotilla arrived at
the riverside Royal Apartments in
Memphis. "And now you must rest, for
tomorrow will be the greatest day of
your life!"

❦CHAPTER TWELVE❧
DRESSED TO THRILL

Julius was woken by a banging on his door. He cuddled up to his pillow even tighter, reluctant to leave the cosiness of his slumber.

"When I go home," he sighed to himself, "the first thing I'm doing is buying myself a big comfy bed. This is PURE heaven."

The banging came again, accompanied by an urgent voice. "Lord Heter, it is time to get up! Your kingdom awaits!"

Just another
five minutes!

Suddenly the door burst open and Imhotep stormed in. "I'm SORRY, Lord Heter," he hissed, "but I must insist that you arise from your bed. Tributes must be paid to the gods before the coronation."

Two women followed Imhotep, carrying decorative gold clothes and jewellery.

"Your ceremonial garments have been prepared, so hop to it." He clapped his hands twice and the women immediately dropped a huge gold garment over Julius's sleepy head.

Then they strapped to his chin a length of tightly plaited hair, that had been interwoven with gold.

"'Ere!" he protested, grabbing the weird sausage-like lump of hair. "What's this?"

"That is your beard, Your Highness," replied Imhotep wearily. "It represents your divinity."

The priest was unimpressed. "That is the very beard that CLEOPATRA wore on her coronation, so I would caution you to be RESPECTFUL!"

At that moment, Cornelius and Felix rushed into the room. Julius was very pleased to see them.

"Hey, Cornelius, did you know that Cleopatra had a BEARD?"

"Of course I did!" replied Cornelius, slightly hurt that Julius was questioning his boundless knowledge.

"THIS IS IT!" cried Julius, pointing excitedly to his ceremonial beard. "This is ACTUALLY Cleopatra's beard!"

With a loud gasp, Imhotep slapped Felix's hoof away. "Do NOT touch the Royal Beard!" Imhotep clapped twice again and the royal dressers scurried obediently out of the room.

The priest grabbed Julius's arm and yanked him off the bed. "This way, Your Highness. Your carriage awaits."

Cornelius scuttled alongside, trying to catch Julius's attention.

"Did Imhotep say anything about your friend the gnu?"

"No, I think we got away with it!" replied Julius.

As Julius was taken out of the palace, he was greeted by a large golden throne which sat upon a great litter held aloft by eight men. Imhotep escorted Julius up to his seat.

A blast of horns filled the air and the grand procession rumbled into life as a stream of soldiers and dignitaries slowly marched along the boulevard, with Julius's throne at the vanguard.

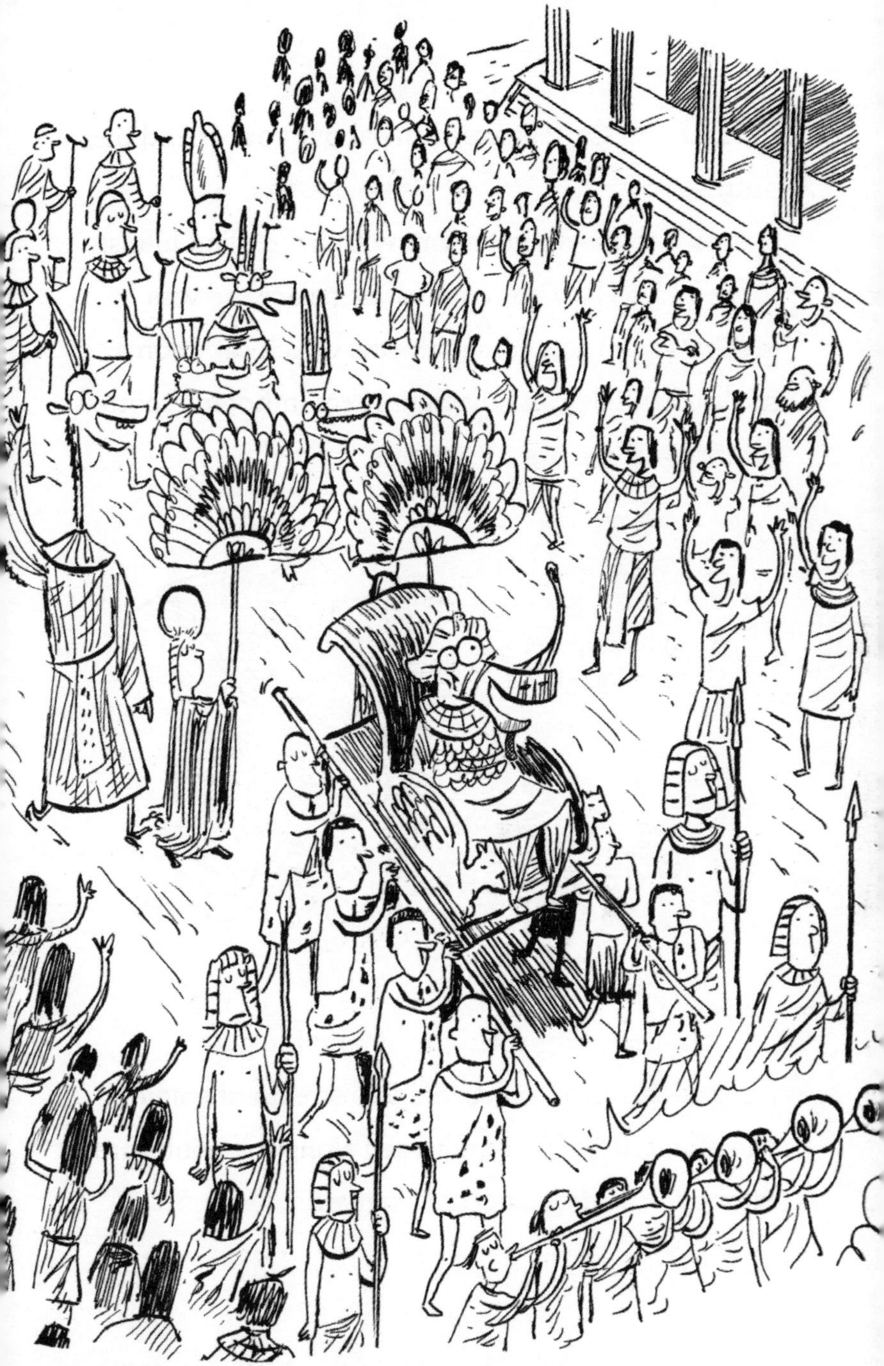

The procession arrived at a very grand-looking temple. Following Imhotep's instructions, Julius dutifully enacted the ancient rituals of paying tribute to the old gods. The priest led him to three temples in all, representing Lower Egypt, Upper Egypt and finally the Two Lands, where Julius laid presents out for the gods and past pharaohs.

Once the formal presentation ceremonies were over, Julius couldn't wait to get back on his mobile throne and head off for the next part. He turned to

Imhotep and clapped his hooves. "What's next? I hope it's more fun than shuffling around boring old temples!"

Imhotep sniffed scornfully, careful to bite his tongue. "Next, Your Highness, we present you to the people of Egypt for your coronation, then we celebrate with a feast."

"Hooray!" cheered Julius. "A feast! Let's make sure we don't miss that!"

"The feast lasts a whole year," replied Imhotep, "so there's little chance of missing it."

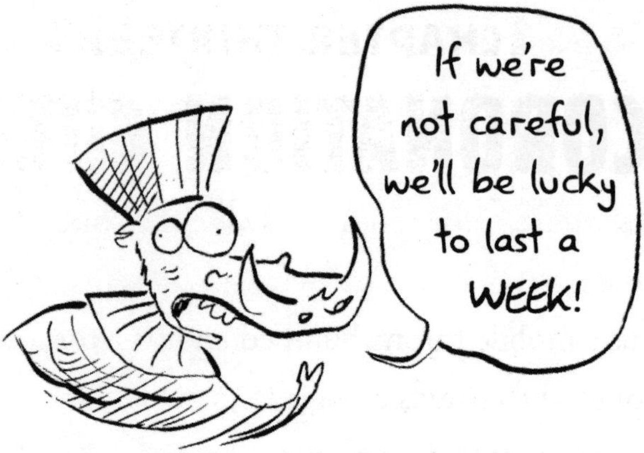
If we're not careful, we'll be lucky to last a WEEK!

❧ CHAPTER THIRTEEN ❧
CORONATION CHEAT

Julius's mobile throne bumped and weaved slowly through the crowds alongside the Nile. Once again he was struck with awe by the pyramids, which loomed large in the background. "Those things really DO touch the sky!" he marvelled.

After a while, the pyramids receded from view and a small rocky valley appeared. Julius was amazed to see colossal ancient statues carved into the mountains themselves, solemnly watching over their procession.

Cor! You can see right up his nostril!

Then, as they made their way around the rocky outcrop, Julius was greeted by the sight of thousands of people and an oddly familiar-looking colossus!

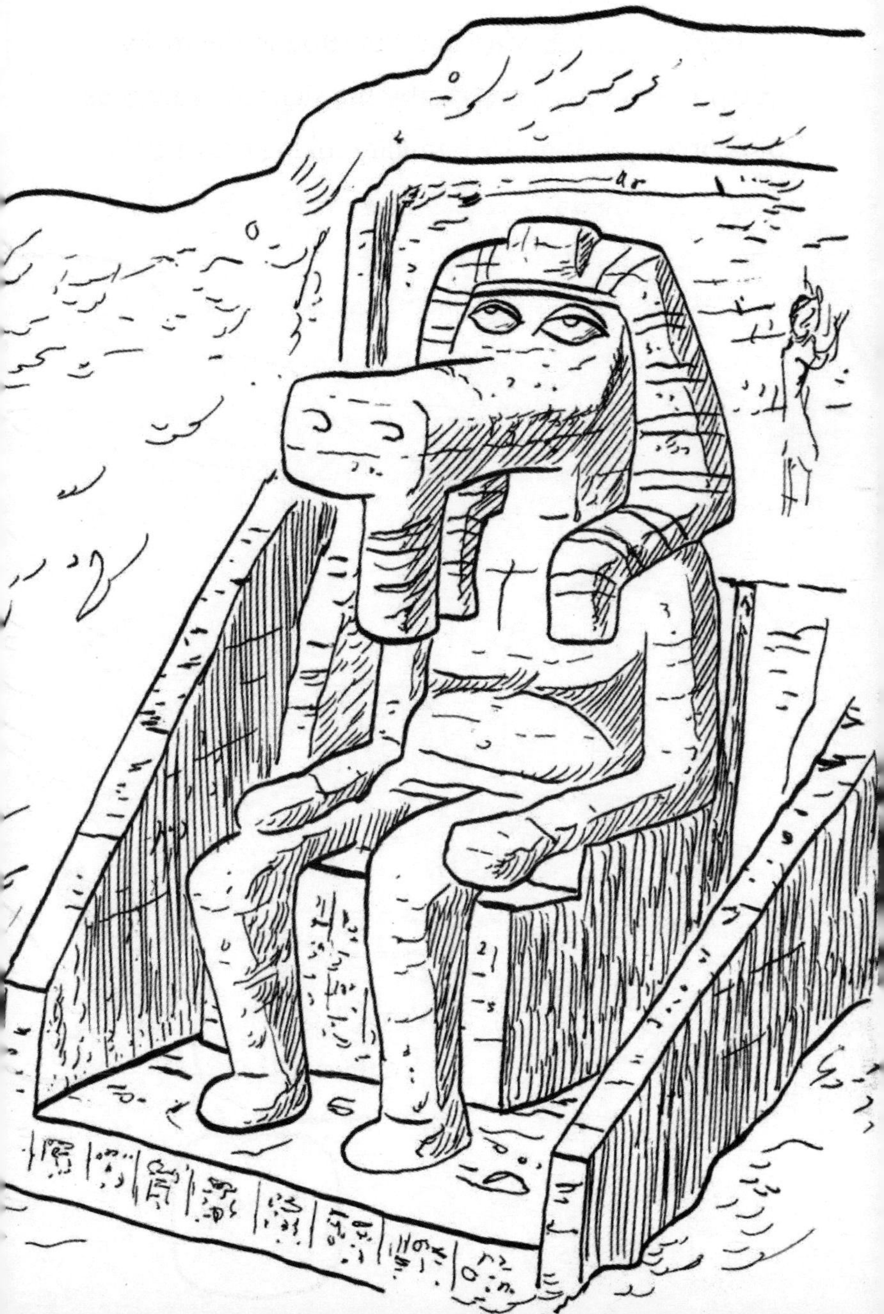

Julius nearly choked; he'd NEVER seen so many people before, not even in the stadia of Rome. Up till now it had all been a bit of jolly fun, but seeing the statue and the sea of faces all staring at him suddenly made it VERY real indeed!

The Egyptians really DID believe he was a god and were expecting him to RULE the country. The WHOLE country! *I've never run a shop, let alone a country,* Julius thought. *WHAT WAS I THINKING?!*

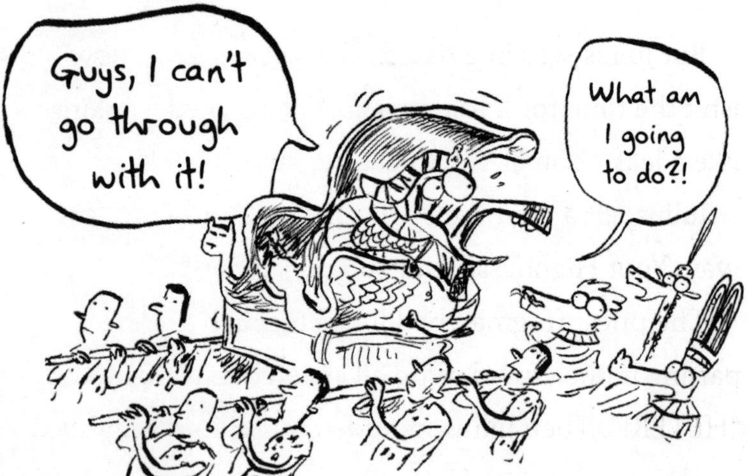
Guys, I can't go through with it!
What am I going to do?!

"It's a bit late to be having second thoughts!" scoffed Milus.

But Julius was in a panic. "Seriously, Milus, now isn't the time for 'I told you so!'" he gasped, shaking like a leaf. "You HAVE to get me out of here!"

Julius felt a tug on his arm. It was Imhotep. "This way, Your Highness. Your subjects await!"

The priest frogmarched Julius through a great parting in the crowd, who all cheered and chanted "HETER!". Then Julius, prodded by Imhotep, climbed up the steps of the giant podium, the deafening roar of the masses in his ears.

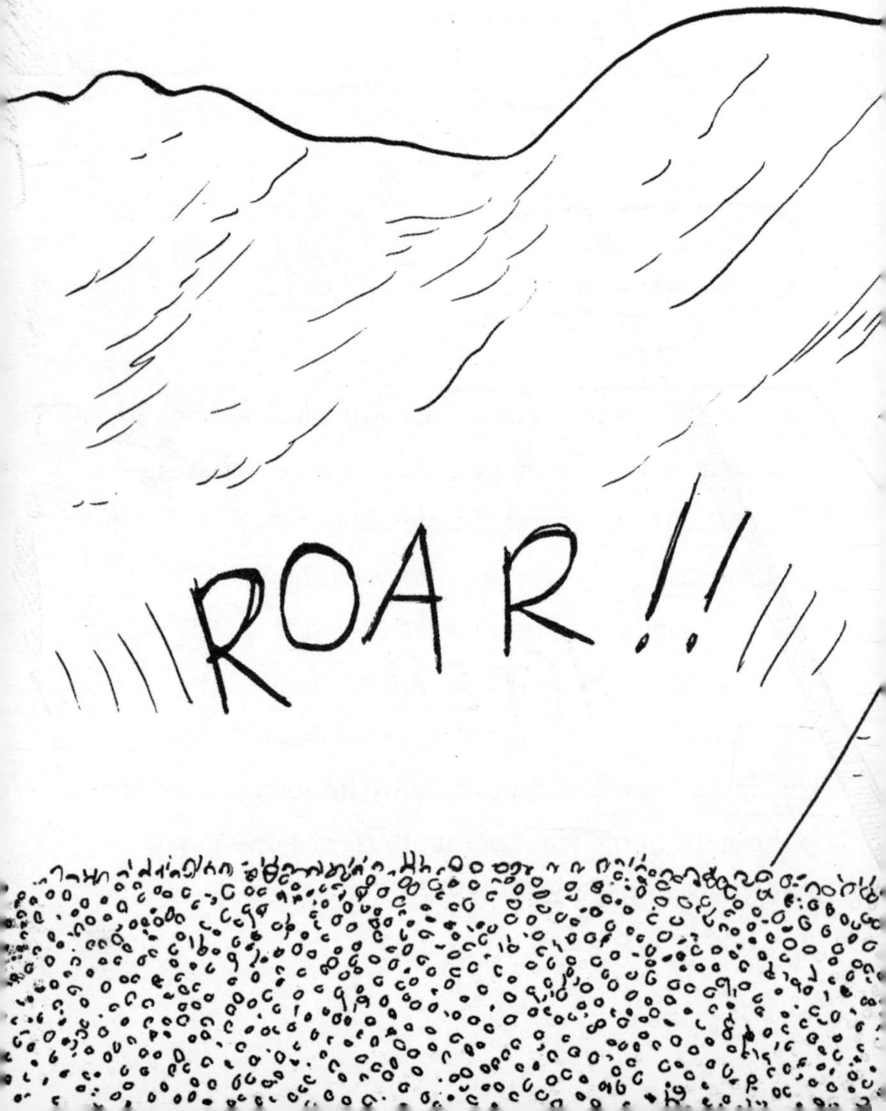
ROAR!!

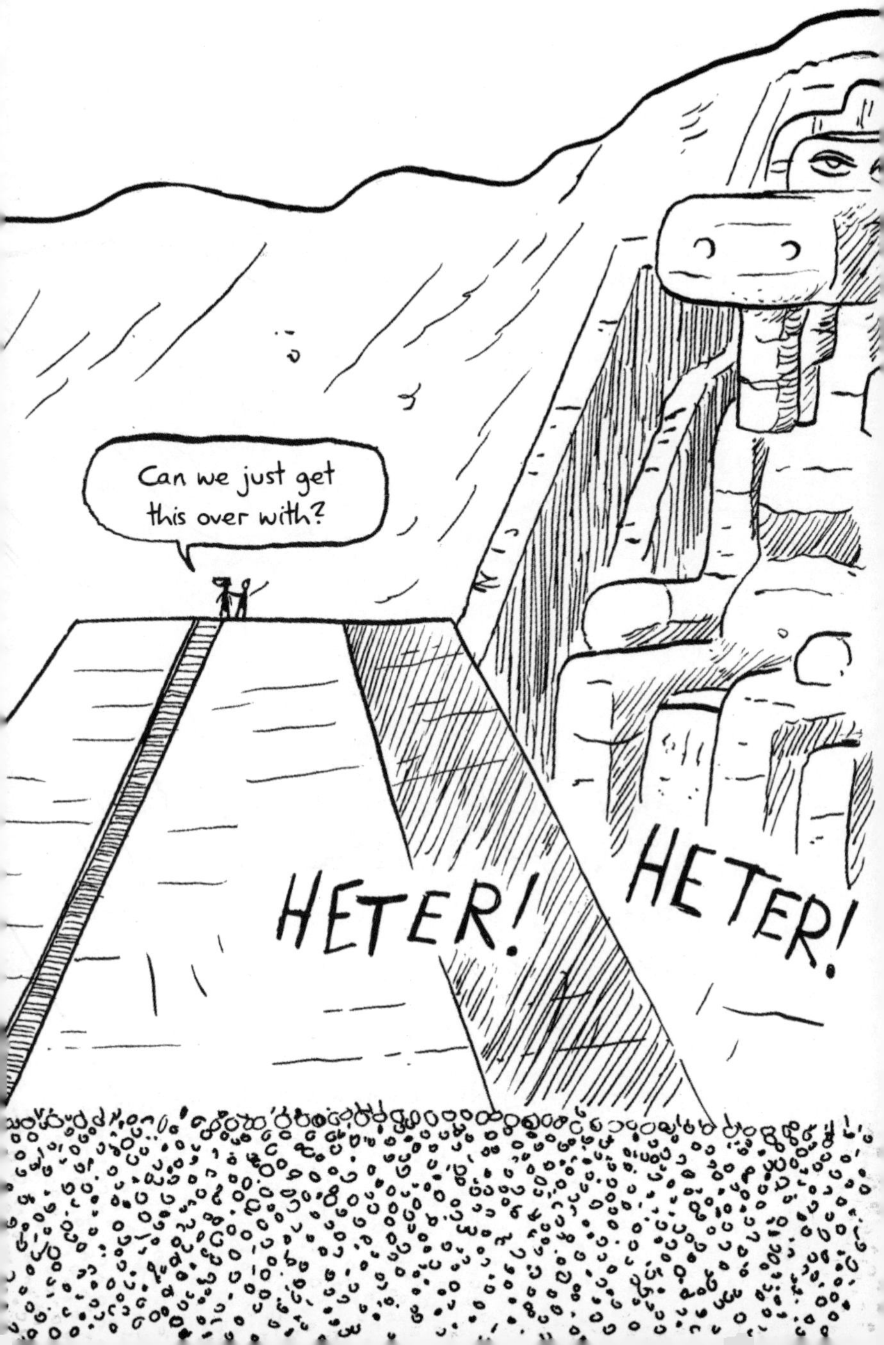
Can we just get this over with?
HETER!
HETER!

From the other side of the podium a troop of priests wearing animal masks appeared, chanting and waving their arms in the air.

"I want to go home now!" sobbed Julius.

The animal priests began splashing water onto the petrified Julius.

Oi! Watch it! Some of that went in my eye!

Imhotep started waving a metal ball on a chain through the air which billowed pungent smoke into Julius's face. "Blargh! Help! Ack!" he coughed. "They're trying to KILL me!"

The priests stood in front of Julius's throne and bowed down to him, each of them mumbling strange words over and over behind their animal masks.

"GOOD WORK, JULIUS!" encouraged Cornelius from the base of the podium. "Stick at it; you're doing brilliantly!"

"But I can't see anything!" wailed Julius. "These idiots threw soapy water in my eyes!"

Julius wiped the water from his eyes, just in time to see a priest wearing a bird's head approach him carrying a weird object.

What are you supposed to be, then? A pigeon?

Ignoring him, the bird priest placed the object on Julius's head.

"What is THAT?" Julius asked. "Some kind of urn?"

Imhotep turned to Julius in disgust. "URN? URN?! Rarely have I heard such IMPUDENCE!" he seethed. "It is your CROWN, you cretin! You bear the symbols of the two ancient Egyptian kingdoms coming together as one!" Shaking with rage, he pointed his finger at Julius. "In all my years I have NEVER heard this sacred artefact referred to as an URN!"

Julius nodded his head approvingly. "Well, you learn something new every day."

Finally the animal priests pushed a stick into each of Julius's front hooves – one a stripy stick with a hook on the end, the other with three sticks swinging from the top.

"And what are THESE?" asked Julius, swinging the sticks about.

"They are the symbols of your authority!" declared Imhotep. "The crook is the symbol of your KINGSHIP, and the flail—"

"Yes," replied the priest, dodging out of the way. "THAT represents the fruitfulness of the land."

Suddenly, at the bottom of the podium, Cornelius leapt up in the air. "THAT'S IT!" he called. "Julius, that's why those soldiers thought you were a god in the first place!"

"Eh? What do you mean?"

"Don't you remember back at the beach? You were holding those two sticks!"

What, like this?

"YES!" cried Cornelius. "Those sticks looked EXACTLY like your crook and flail!"

Julius slapped his forehead with his hoof. "THAT'S why they thought I was a god!" he laughed.

Perplexed, Imhotep put his hands on his hips. "What are you blathering on about?"

"Oh, er ... nothing..." blustered Julius, hiding the sticks behind his back. "Let's just carry on and get this over with, shall we?"

Imhotep took Julius by the hoof and presented him to the crowd. "SONS AND DAUGHTERS OF EGYPT, I GIVE TO YOU YOUR NEW KING, HETER!"

CHAPTER FOURTEEN
TOMB RAIDER

Now that I have been officially crowned the horse god, we can EAT LIKE KINGS!

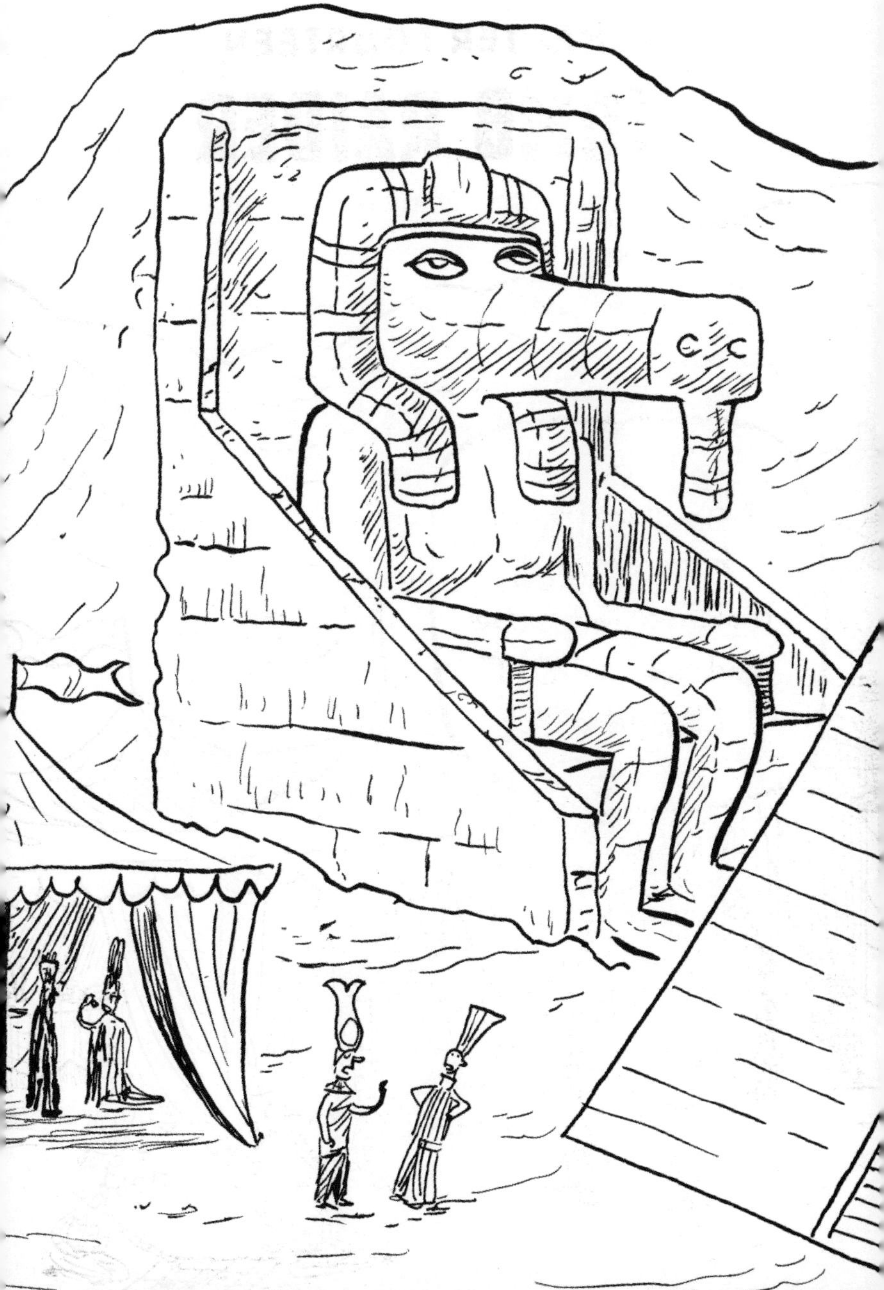

"Right!" said Julius proudly. "I think that went pretty well, all told!" He put his arm round his brother, who was deep in a game of Ludus with Rufus. "Did you see me up there?" he said. "Didn't I look brilliant!"

"Up where?" asked Brutus, not glancing up from his game.

"ON THE PODIUM!" Julius blurted.

I'M now officially PHARAOH!

"Oh, that's nice," replied Brutus, pretending to be disinterested.

"Pff!" complained Julius, plopping down on his seat grumpily.

"Well done, Julius," said Lucia, patting him on the arm. "I thought you were very brave up there!"

Pliny walked over chomping on a big lobster claw. "Good work, Debra," he slurped. "You smell proper fragrant too."

Just so you know, the lobster here is AMAZING!

"You played it well, donkey," admitted Milus, nibbling on a honey-covered mouse. "You've been lucky so far, but we should leave before our cover is blown."

"Milus is right," Cornelius agreed. "The longer we stay, the deeper the trouble we're in."

Suddenly Julius did a double take and sprang up from his chair. "Hey! Wait a minute, where's Felix? I haven't seen him since the coronation!"

"THAT STUPID ANTELOPE!" Milus roared, pulling at his mane in frustration.

Julius quickly put his hoof over the lion's mouth. "SHH!" he hissed. "Let's not draw attention to ourselves!"

Batting away the zebra's hoof, Milus glared at Julius. "Just try sticking your hoof over my mouth again and see what happens!"

A familiar voice interrupted them. "Cor blimey! I leave you for five minutes and you're already trying to kill one another!"

Everyone spun round to see Felix standing in front of them, bold as brass.

"And where have you been?" scolded Julius.

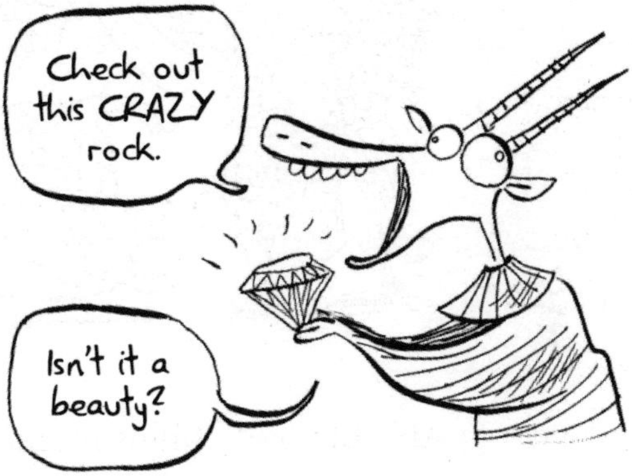
Check out this CRAZY rock.
Isn't it a beauty?

Cornelius took a closer look at the big blue gem, his eyes nearly popping out. "Felix! WHERE did you find this?!"

"It was in a cave back there," he said, pointing behind him. He lowered his voice to a whisper and beckoned everyone closer. "The place was FULL of treasure!"

"Ooh, a tomb..." repeated Felix blankly, not really knowing what that meant.

"Yes, a tomb!" replied Cornelius. "Ancient pharaohs would keep all their prized possessions in there along with their sarcophagus."

Felix's mouth dropped open.

"A COFFIN, before you ask," said Cornelius.

"Yeah, I know!" huffed Felix. "I was just yawning." And he opened his mouth even wider, stretched his arms and made a big yawny sound like a cow falling down a hole.

So! Not only am I a brilliant rock collector, but I'm also a master tomb raider!

"Yeah, I'm not sure that's something you wanna go shouting about!" snarled Pliny, spitting out an expensive prawn tail.

Felix popped the jewel back into his knapsack and patted it shut. "Righto! What are we all doing then? Lots of eating and drinking?"

"No!" cried Cornelius, wrestling the knapsack away from Felix. "You can't just steal stuff from pharaohs' tombs!"

What about THE CURSE!

Pliny shook his head in despair. "What curse?" he scoffed. "The hairy piglet's gone bonkers!"

"No, it's true!" said Cornelius. "Pharaohs protect their tombs with terrible curses to deter thieves. If you don't put it back, we'll all die really horribly!"

Blimey, WHATEVER we do here seems to mean certain death!

Julius patted Felix on his shoulder. "Come on, Cornelius is right; we'd better put it back. I'm quite keen to live a long jolly life, thank you very much!"

Poor Felix looked forlorn.

"Don't worry, Felix, there are plenty of rocks lying around that will be JUST as great, trust me!"

"Not like this one," sighed the antelope.

Julius turned to his friends. "The rest of you wait here for five minutes, while Cornelius and I make sure Felix puts this back."

CHAPTER FIFTEEN
CHAMBER OF HORRORS

Julius, Cornelius and Felix sneaked out through a flap at the back of the tent and scurried over to the feet of the giant statue of Heter.

"OK," said Cornelius. "Which way now?"

Felix scoured the landscape to get his bearings. "This way!" he announced confidently and scooted off towards the far end of the rocky outcrop.

Here it is, by this tiled floor!

Julius was impressed. "Cor, you're very brave!"

"How do you mean?" asked Felix.

"Well," said Julius, peering into the hole, "it's very dark in there. I wouldn't have gone in on my own!"

Cornelius gave Felix a little nudge. "Go on then, show us the way!"

Felix stepped to one side. "I'm not going down there NOW!" he protested. "Not after all your talk of curses and stuff!"

Cornelius gave the antelope a big shove. "There WON'T be a curse if you put it back!"

With a big "TUT!" Felix had a rummage in his knapsack and pulled out a tiny oil lamp.

He quickly bashed his little metal fire striker against his pocket flint and lit the wick with the sparks.

"Impressive!" said Julius.

Julius and Cornelius followed Felix as he gingerly tiptoed down the steps. When they finally reached the bottom, they found a door covered in strange oval markings. Cornelius's eyes nearly popped out.

"Cartouches!" he cried.

"Bless you!" replied Julius.

"No!" said Cornelius. "Cartouches are the Egyptian symbol to denote a pharaoh. You really did find an ancient royal tomb!"

Julius pushed his shoulder against the door. "And we really ought to be putting back what we shouldn't take!" he huffed.

As the door creaked open, a gust of air whistled past them, blowing out Felix's lamp.

Well, that's a bit annoying!

They squeezed through the tight gap between the door and the wall into a cold, musty, pitch-black room.

"Hurry up, Felix!" urged Julius. "Get that lamp lit. This place is starting to give me the creeps!"

Felix bashed hard at his flint. "Come on, come on!" he huffed impatiently under his breath. Finally, with one big chip at his flint, the tiny sparks lit the small wick. "Got it!" he declared.

But Julius and Cornelius weren't listening.

"By the gods," whispered Cornelius, his jaw hitting the floor, "what IS this place?"

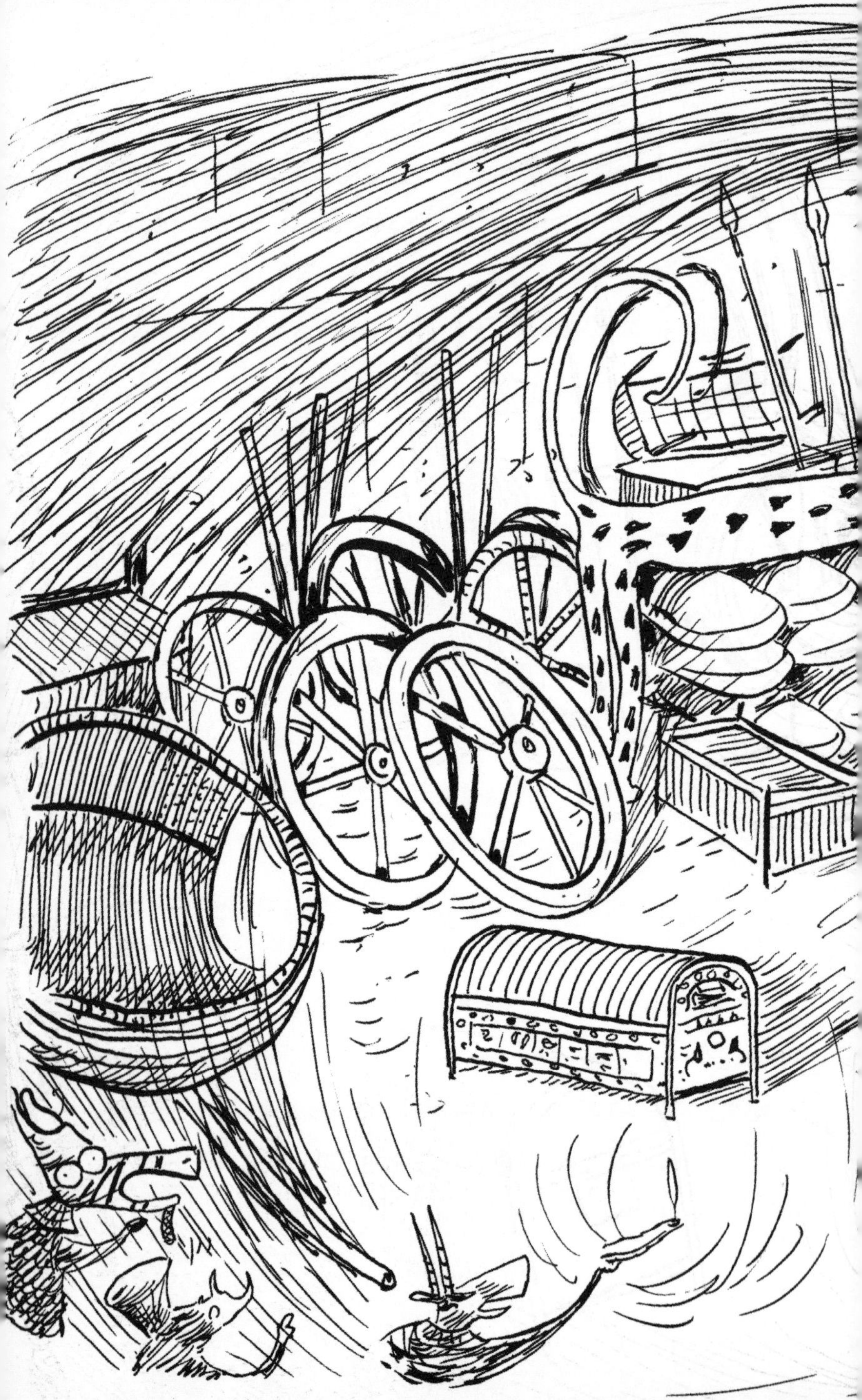

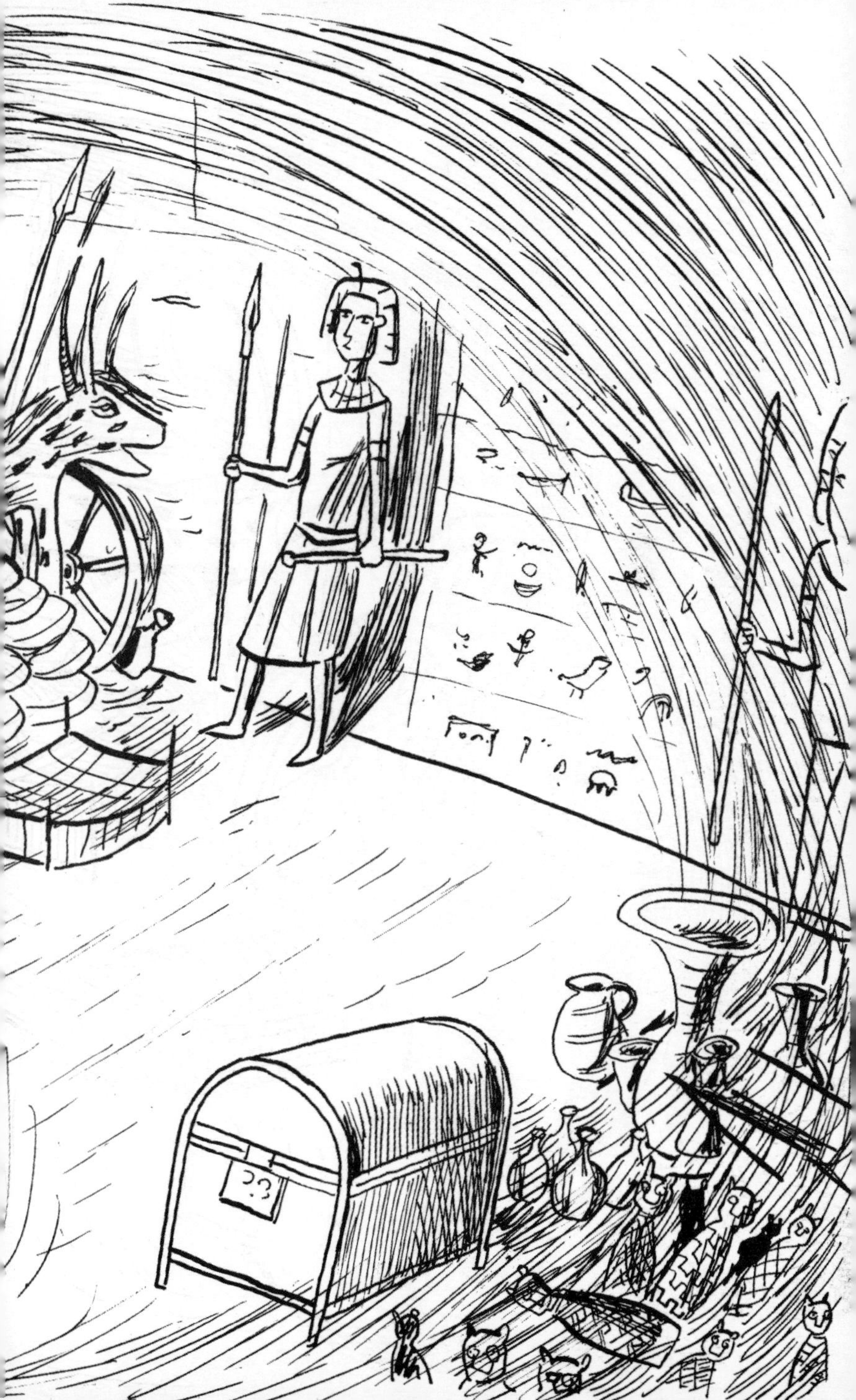

Cornelius dragged Felix and his lamp over to one of the walls. "Look at these images; the colours are as fresh as the day they were painted!"

Julius held up a statuette. "All this stuff – golden chairs, chariot wheels, pots – what's it all for?"

"Whoever's chamber this is," replied Cornelius, scrutinizing a small pot carefully, "this is the stuff they were taking with them into the afterlife!"

Felix let out a little squeal. "'Ere! There's loads of cats in here! LOOK!"

"Mummies," whispered Cornelius.

"I don't care WHOSE they are," cried Felix. "I don't like 'em!"

Julius was examining two big statues. "Hey, Felix, bring your lamp over here. Look at these giants next to this door!"

Cornelius rushed up and placed his little hooves on the door. "They ARE guards!" he declared. "And they're probably guarding another chamber!"

Julius gave the door a big shove with his shoulder.

"What are you doing?!" exclaimed Cornelius.

"Opening the door! What does it look like?"

Cornelius dived in front of the door protectively. "But you CAN'T!" shouted the little warthog. "That's probably where the TOMB is!"

"And?" demanded Julius indignantly. "Don't you want to know who's in there?"

"You can't DISTURB the tomb!" cried Cornelius in horror, and he spread his arms wide.

"Let's just put the stone back and leg it!" he said.

Felix came up and leant on the door. "I promise to put the stone back if you let us look behind this door."

And with that, they all HEAVED on the heavy door. As it creaked open, the light from Felix's lamp glinted off something very big and VERY golden inside.

"Look, it even has a face painted on it!" cried Julius.

"Who's this chap, then?" asked Felix.

"What do you mean?" replied Cornelius, distractedly.

Felix held up his light. "In this *other* sarcophagus!"

Julius examined the second casket, which was
also covered in delicate patterns and hieroglyphics.
Then something caught his eye. "Wait! Look at these
markings. Aren't they ROMAN NUMERALS?"

Cornelius leapt to Julius's side to take a look and,
sure enough, carved in blue against the gold were the
very familiar markings of Roman numerals.

"Well spotted, Julius!" he praised. Cornelius studied
the face on the sarcophagus and let out a little gasp.
"And you're right too, Felix! The chap in here is
definitely NOT Egyptian. He's a ROMAN!"

Cornelius stood back from the coffin in awe. "Which can mean only one thing..." he whispered.

This is the LOST tomb of Cleopatra and Mark Antony!

"Oh, goody!" Felix clapped. "They'll be pleased we found it again!"

"No, they WON'T!" scolded Cornelius. "They'll be FURIOUS!"

"But who are Cleo Claptrap and Mark Anchovy?" asked Julius.

"Cleo*patra*," replied Cornelius, "was the last pharaoh of Egypt. Mark Antony was her Roman lover. They were defeated by Julius Caesar more than a hundred and fifty years ago, bringing to an end the age of the pharaohs."

"Well, until I came along!" said Julius proudly.

Cornelius grabbed Felix's knapsack. "Look, these tombs are SACRED and we really shouldn't be here!" he cried. "Put the stone back, Felix, and let's leave now!"

Felix wrenched his bag out of Cornelius's hooves. "NO, CORNELIUS, YOU CAN'T MAKE ME! I DON'T CARE ABOUT YOUR STUPID CURSES!!" he bawled. "I'M KEEPING MY SHINY STONE, SO THERE!!"

With that, Felix blew out his lamp and vanished into the dark.

{CHAPTER SIXTEEN}
DON'T RAIN ON MY PARADE

Julius and Cornelius scrambled out of the pitch-black tomb and into the blinding glare of daylight.

"That idiotic antelope!" fumed Cornelius, shielding his eyes. "He'll be the death of us!"

Julius patted him on the back. "Don't be so hard on him. He's just passionate about his rocks, that's all!"

"If my head drops off because that fool's put a curse on us, I'll be FURIOUS!" raged Cornelius.

They soon reached the big tent where the party was in full swing and sneaked back in through their secret flap.

"He can't have got far!" reasoned Julius.

"Felix!" Julius answered, wafting the stench of the seaweed away from his nostrils. "He's run off with his stupid gem."

"Never mind all that!" spluttered Brutus, putting his arm round his brother. "You and me need to TALK!"

Brutus gently ruffled Julius's mane. "When are you going to make me a god too? Eh?"

Julius shrugged Brutus's arm off. "What do you mean?"

"Oh, come on, Julius," pleaded Brutus, throwing his arms in the air. "WE'RE BROTHERS!"

Julius shoved his hoof in front of Brutus's mouth. "Hush!" he hissed. "Look, they don't dish out their godhoods willy-nilly. You have to EARN it!"

"EARN IT?!" jeered Brutus, pushing Julius away. "What have YOU done to EARN IT?"

Julius tried desperately to quieten his brother. "Brutus, please!"

But Brutus was getting redder with anger, swaggering about and waving his arms. "This whole thing is RIDICULOUS!" he sneered loudly.

Some of the dignitaries were now looking round, irritated by the disturbance.

"They all think you're a HORSE god!" he shouted.

But you're not even a horse, you're a ZEBRA!

Julius clamped a hoof over Brutus's mouth. "Please be QUIET!" he insisted. "You've eaten too many lobsters and it's gone to your head!"

Julius became aware that someone was standing right behind him. He spun round to find the frowning face of Imhotep the priest.

"Is there a problem?" he hissed menacingly.

Julius let go of Brutus, dropping him to the floor, then put his arms behind his back, looking the picture of innocence.

"Good," said Imhotep. "We've been looking for you. Your presence is needed once more." He gazed for a few seconds at Brutus, who was sitting on the floor rubbing his head, then eyed Julius suspiciously before letting out a big "Humph!" He turned on his sandals and walked briskly away. "Follow me, 'horse'!"

Julius glared at Brutus angrily. "Now you've done it!" he snapped. "Imhotep probably *heard* you!"

"Oh, who cares?" huffed Brutus grumpily.

Before he could say any more, Julius was whisked away out of the tent and back to the great podium where his coronation had taken place. Imhotep impatiently waved Julius towards the rear stairs that led to the summit.

As Imhotep shoved him up the steps, Julius began to panic. "But I'm not ready!" he protested. "I need my special adviser, Cornelius!"

The priest glared at the whimpering zebra. "Your friend is not with you this time, horse," he snarled. "Besides, you are a god; you do not need the advice of mere mortals!"

Julius poked his head over the summit. A great cheer went up as the crowd spotted his crown and familiar face. With a big gulp, Julius stepped fully into view on the podium, waving his hooves at his adoring fans.

Julius tried to address the cheering masses, but he could barely hear *himself* shout above the roar! As he waved, he suddenly realized that his fans had stopped chanting "Heter". *What on earth are they shouting now?* he thought.

He leant towards them and put his hoof to his ear. "YOU WHAT?!!" he yelled.

Julius realized with horror what they were saying and held up his hooves. The crowd fell silent.

"I'M AFRAID I CAN'T MAKE IT RAIN TODAY!"

The crowd became restless and started to boo. Julius panicked. He spotted Imhotep at the foot of the steps looking up at him, arms folded and foot tapping impatiently.

"OK, OK!" he said, turning back to the crowd.

It happened on cue before, he reasoned to himself, *so why shouldn't it happen again?* He raised both his arms high in the air and closed his eyes.

There was a long silence as everyone looked to the heavens, waiting expectantly for any sign of rain.

Nothing.

Julius slowly opened his eyes to see clear blue skies. If anything, it was sunnier than before he'd started this charade.

The crowd began chanting again.

Julius held up his hooves apologetically. "I'M SORRY!" he shouted. "BUT I DON'T THINK IT'S GOING TO HAPPEN TODAY!"

This was NOT what they wanted to hear! The sound of boos rippled through the crowd again. Pieces of food were thrown at Julius.

Julius grew frightened as his adoring fans turned into an angry mob, and he started to edge backwards.

Suddenly he noticed a solitary figure break through the crowd and climb up one of the steps at the front.

"HE'S NOT A HORSE!" called out the mysterious figure.

Julius leant over to try to get a better glimpse of the speaker. *It looks like a GNU*, he thought.

The gnu called up to Julius. "IT IS YOU!" she cried. "JULIUS ZEBRA!"

Julius dived to the floor. *It's that gnu again! What am I going to do?* he thought. *I need to get out of here!*

He became aware of a pair of sandalled feet directly in front of his nose.

"AS I SUSPECTED!"

Julius timidly peeked up to see the twisted, angry face of Imhotep the priest.

Julius scrambled to his hooves. "Listen, it's not what you think!" he pleaded.

"I'm not listening to YOU!" spat the priest. He beckoned to some nearby guards to grab the zebra. "You are a CHARLATAN!" He leant in close to Julius as the guards prepared to drag him away. "And Egypt does NOT look favourably upon CHARLATANS!"

As Imhotep gestured to the guards to take him away, a familiar-looking crocodile leapt into their path. "LUCIA!" cried Julius.

\{ CHAPTER SEVENTEEN \}
HORSING AROUND

Lucia skipped over gleefully to the chariot and tugged at the reins to make sure they were tightly fastened.

"Lucia, this time you've gone TOO FAR!" railed Julius. "You've finally gone CRACKERS!"

Lucia patted Julius on the head. "Quiet now, Julius," she soothed. "What better way to prove once

and for all that you're a horse, than by winning a
CHARIOT RACE?"

Julius let out a big huff. "One, don't pat the Royal
Head, thank you; and two, I'd rather be strapped to
ANYONE other than this stinky imbecile!"

Brutus ignored him and brushed his beloved mop
of seaweed, disturbing a dozen flies as he did so.

Lucia skipped up onto the carriage, where her
charioteer partner, Rufus, waited patiently. "Have
faith in your brother!" she urged with a laugh.

With your zebra
speed and my
superior chariot-
racing skills, this
race will be a
no-brainer!

Brutus grinned smugly at Julius. "See, bruv? People think we're GREAT together!"

The rest of the gang arrived to wish them luck. Cornelius patted Julius on the head. "Good luck, chaps; there's only one winner in this race!"

Julius now turned his anger on Felix who was meekly hiding behind Cornelius. "This is all your fault, Felix!" he fumed. "You've put a curse on me ever since you pinched that stupid stone!"

Felix hid a little bit further behind the warthog.

Also looking on were Milus and Pliny, sitting disgruntled on a rock.

One could argue that since I met YOU, donkey, my life has been cursed!

Pliny jumped up and stood in front of the two zebras. "Ignore that grump!" he said. "But listen to Lucia. Old teeth-face is RIGHT!"

The little mouse hopped about as if he were a horse zipping around a race track. "You zebras have hooves of FIRE!"

Julius looked at his front left hoof. "We do?"

"YES!" replied Pliny. He pointed to the horses next to them. "Forget those mollycoddled nags; when's the last time they were chased by a hungry lion?"

Julius watched as their rivals were harnessed to their chariot. Two great muscular horses, they looked powerful enough to take on the whole Roman army!

Maybe never, but I still wouldn't mess with 'em!

"Have you seen who their charioteer is?" added Cornelius.

IMHOTEP!!

"Word is," said Cornelius, "that before he became a priest, he was a champion chariot racer in his youth!"

"Well, that's THAT then!" sighed Julius despondently. "We're DEFINITELY doomed."

Pliny leapt onto Julius's head and eyeballed him. "Now, that ain't the talk of a ROMAN CHAMPION!" He backflipped off Julius's head and deftly landed on his little feet. He gave Julius's hoof a big kick. "You might have feet of fire..."

But you also need some FIRE in your belly!

A big smile spread across Brutus's face. "That's where I come in!" He grinned. "I had some very spicy food at that party and it's proper set MY belly on fire!"

Julius creased up his nose. "I don't want to know!"

Lucia tugged on the reins for a final test of the buckles. "That's it!" she announced. "We're ready to go!"

They trotted over to the starting line as Pliny and the others scurried to the sidelines and found themselves a good spot to watch the race from.

The two chariots stood side by side, ready for the final signal. Julius looked over at Imhotep, who bared his teeth and growled.

"We're all going to die!" whimpered Julius.

"Don't worry, chaps," Lucia said confidently. "I've watched hundreds of these races. I know EXACTLY what I'm doing."

"I flippin' hope so!" Julius burbled. "We're all for the chop if we lose!"

"Just don't do anything STUPID!" Julius begged.

But, before Brutus had a chance to reply, the gong rang out and the chariots were OFF!

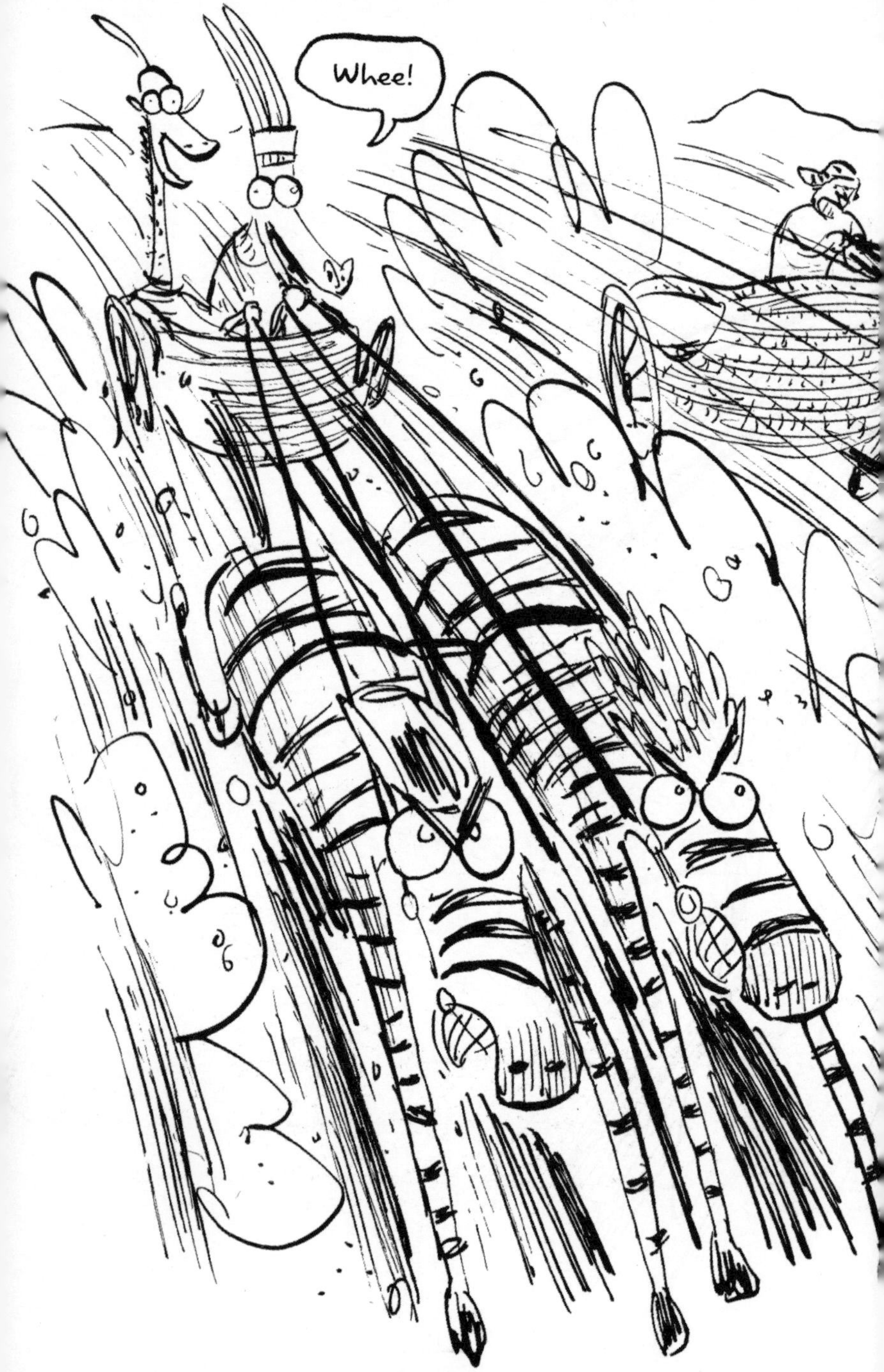
Whee!

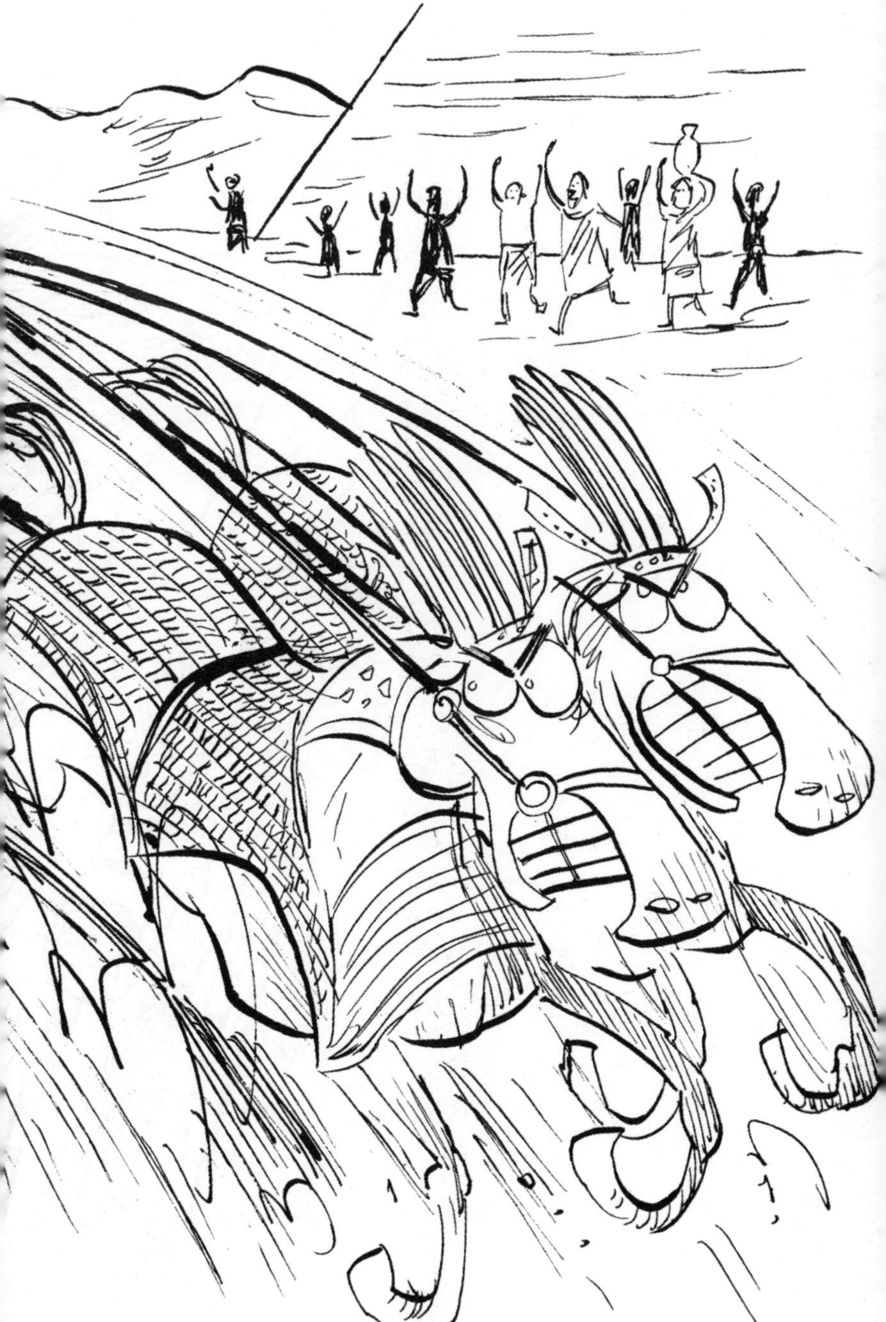

Their lives at stake, Julius and Brutus galloped at top speed. In the chariot, Lucia nimbly held the reins, carefully steering them around the tight bends.

But Imhotep was fast too! The powerful Egyptian horses ferociously pounded their hooves into the hot sand, easily whisking the priest past the two zebras.

Julius and Brutus put their heads down, picked up the pace and pushed every sinew and muscle to the limit. Lucia clung on tightly, tugging the reins sharply as they approached the next turn. They screeched round in a great cloud of dust and sand, almost clipping the Great Pyramid itself.

They had taken the corner too fast! The chariot careened onto one wheel, nearly tipping Lucia and Rufus out. But Rufus grabbed hold of the chariot with one hoof and Lucia with the other, and they managed to keep Julius and Brutus on track!

"He's getting away!" yelled Julius. "Come on, Brutus. RUN FASTER!"

With an extra burst they caught up with Imhotep.

The priest didn't like this one bit; taking out his spear, he tried to ram it into Lucia's wheel!

"YOU DIRTY CHEAT!" roared Rufus, waving his hoof angrily. "If baldy had stuck his spear into our spokes, we'd have HAD it!"

Lucia kept her focus on the track ahead. "Get ready if he comes again!" she ordered. "We NEED to pull ahead!"

"HOW MANY TIMES DO WE HAVE TO GO ROUND?" Brutus puffed.

"THREE TIMES!" she replied.

"AND HOW MANY TIMES HAVE WE BEEN ROUND ALREADY?" Brutus shouted.

"NEARLY ONCE!" cried Lucia.

But Julius was easily keeping up the pace. "Stick with it, brother!" he gasped. "If being a gladiator has given me one thing, it's stamina!"

Thanks to Julius's pace and Lucia's steady steering, they were soon gaining on Imhotep's chariot once more.

"NOW LET'S TRY TO GET PAST WITHOUT GIVING THEM A CHANCE TO TAKE US OUT!" cried Julius.

"Don't worry," replied Brutus with a cheeky grin. "I've got a better idea!" And with that he PULLED the chariot right into the path of the Egyptians!

The Egyptian chariot bounced dangerously into the air as it was shoved off course, but the experienced Imhotep somehow kept it all in one piece on the track.

"WOOHOOHOOO!" laughed Brutus. "THAT SHOWED 'EM!"

"You FLIPPIN' IDIOT!" screamed Julius. "You nearly took us ALL out!"

Brutus took no notice of his brother. "Oh, stop being such a wimp! Chariot racing is SUPPOSED to be dangerous!"

Julius risked a sideways glance at Brutus. "Well, more fool you! You're the one who lost his stupid wig in the melee!"

"WE HAVE TO GO BACK FOR IT!" howled Brutus, desperately looking behind.

"We'll get it on the next circuit!" said Julius.

"Then we'd better HURRY!" And Brutus burst forward with renewed energy, pulling the chariot faster than ever before.

The spectators went wild as Julius's chariot zipped past Imhotep and round the next bend.

The chariot hurtled down the next straight and round the final corner. In the distance Brutus spied his beloved green locks. "THERE IT IS!" he exclaimed.

Cor! You really love that wig, don't you!

But as Brutus twisted the racing chariot towards the clump of seaweed, he clattered his hooves into Julius.

"CAREFUL!" yelped Julius, as he felt his legs crumple underneath him. He tried to steady himself, but it was too late.

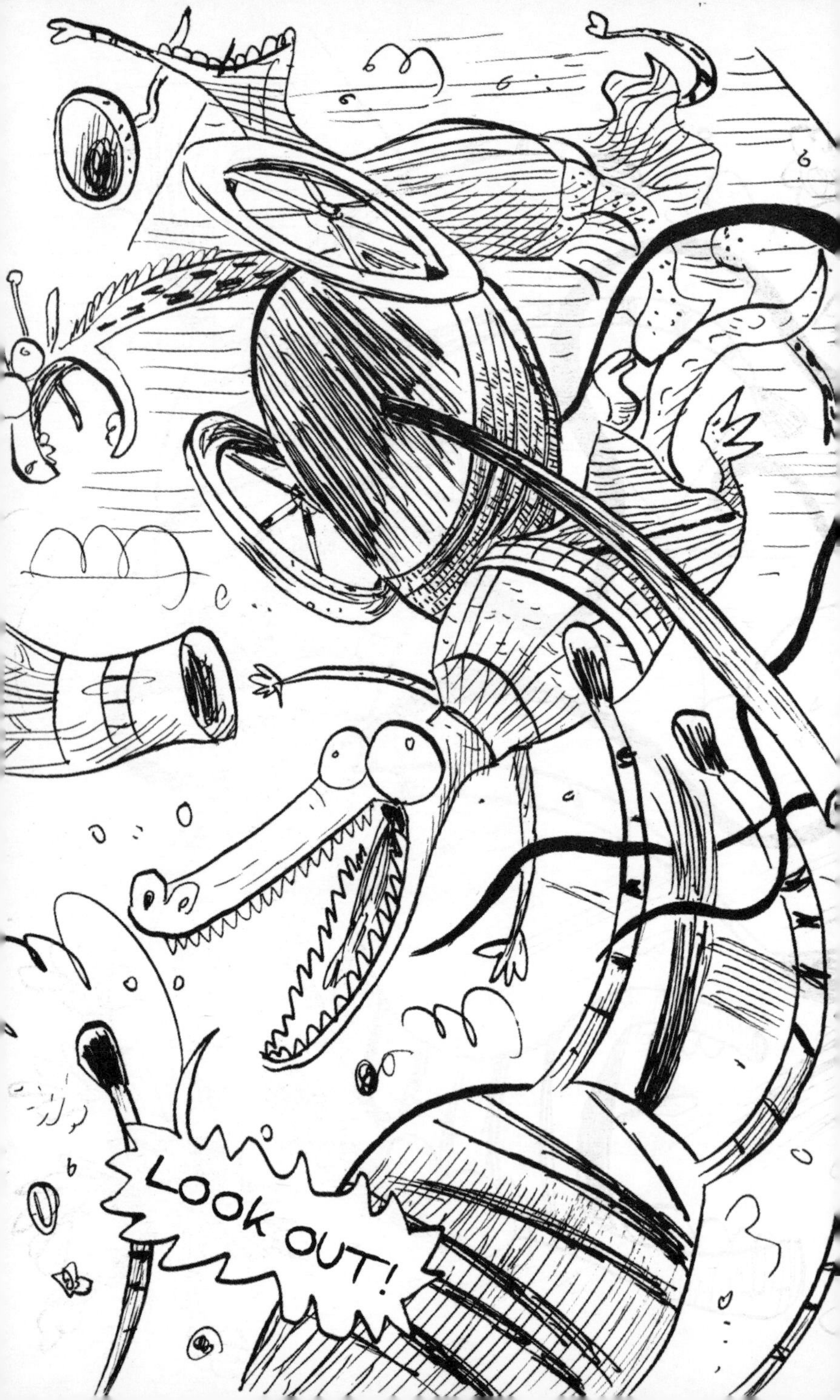
LOOK OUT!

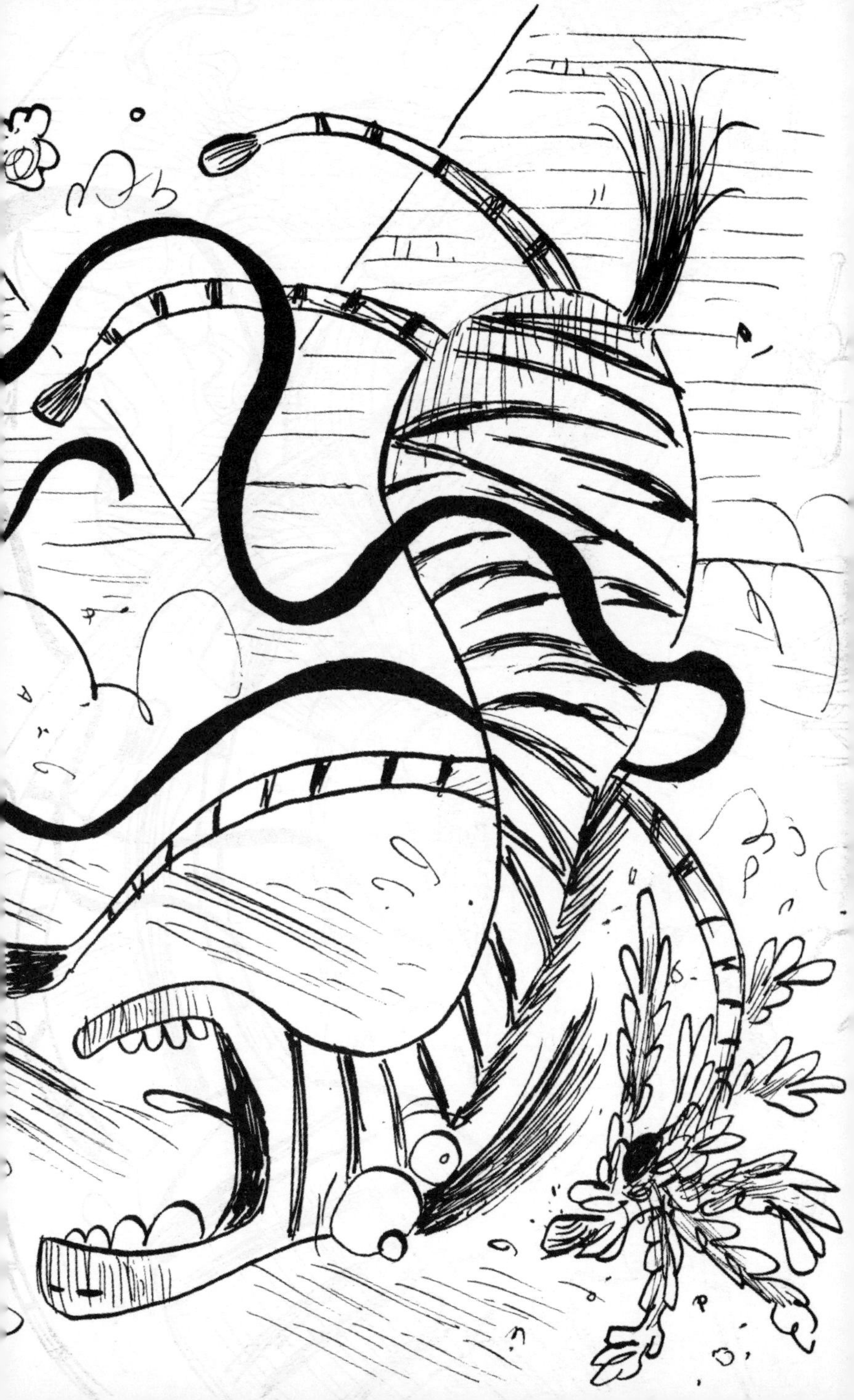

As the dust settled, Julius wondered if he was still alive. Then a pungent, fishy stench wafted up his nostrils. Yes, he was very much alive.

Julius was just about to berate his imbecilic brother, when the rush and thunder of Imhotep's chariot speeding on past took his breath away. In the distance the chariot crossed the finishing line to great cheers and applause.

"Brilliant," said Julius, and he flopped back to the ground, exhausted.

CHAPTER EIGHTEEN
THE GAME'S UP!

Lucia jumped out from the overturned chariot and rushed over to Julius. "Are you all right?" she cried.

"I ... I think so," he mumbled, rubbing his elbow. "Just a couple of grazes."

Julius's friends came running over, fearful of their plight.

What happened? You took a turn for the worse!

"It was THIS bonehead!" growled Julius, thumbing his hoof towards his brother. "He pulled us all over trying to get his WIG!"

Well, I got it, didn't I?

"I'll give him more than a wig if someone doesn't stop me!" vowed Julius, lunging at his brother.

But before he could make good his threat, a cry of "ARREST THEM!" rang out across the makeshift arena.

Flanked by a small group of soldiers, Imhotep stormed over, tossing his helmet into the sand.

"Uh-oh," warned Cornelius. "Now we're for it!"

Julius gingerly pulled himself up and attempted to reason with the furious priest. "Look! This proves nothing!" he argued, waving his hooves wildly. "Let me race on my own, unhindered by my useless brother. I'll PROVE to you that I'm a god!"

But, as Julius waved his arms around, Imhotep let out a great, theatrical gasp and took a step back.

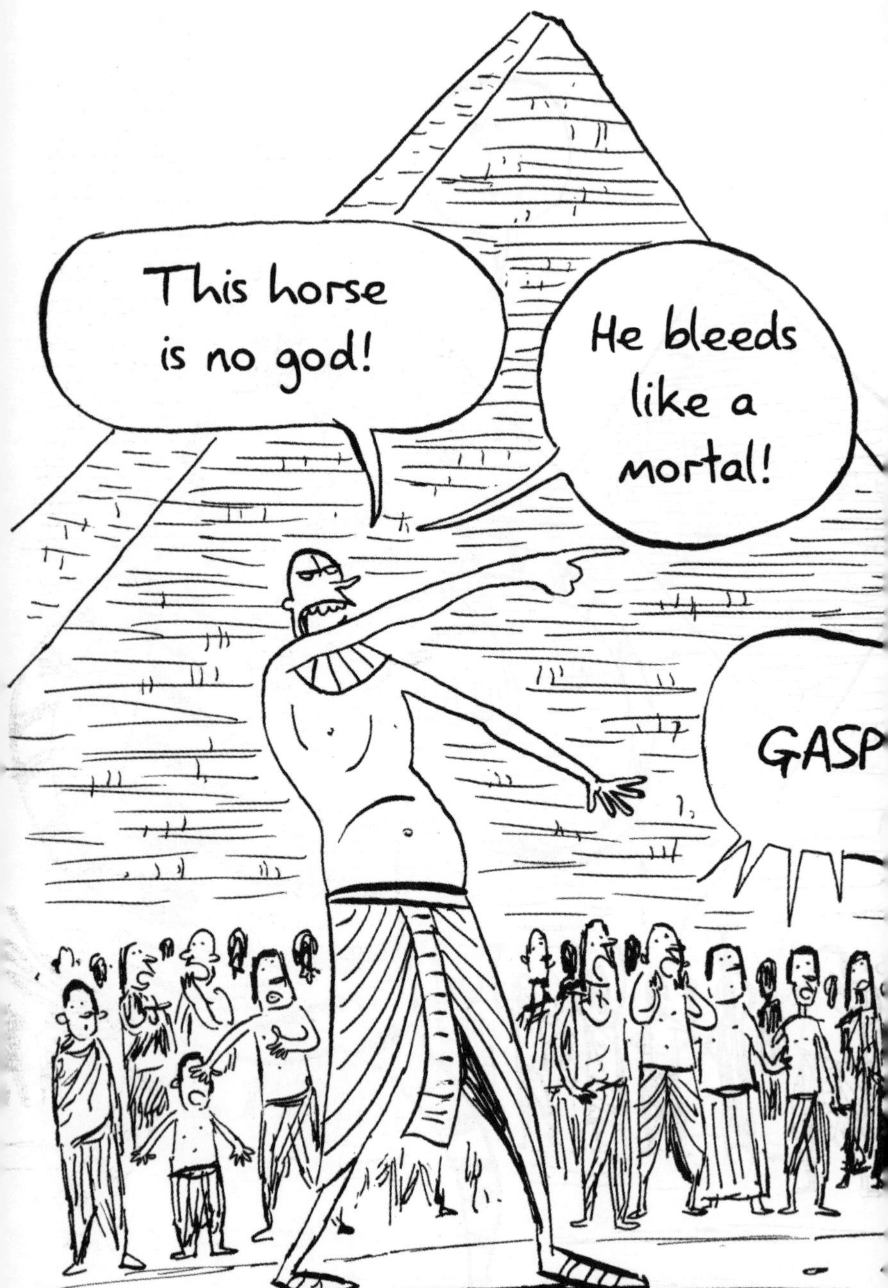
This horse is no god!
He bleeds like a mortal!
GASP

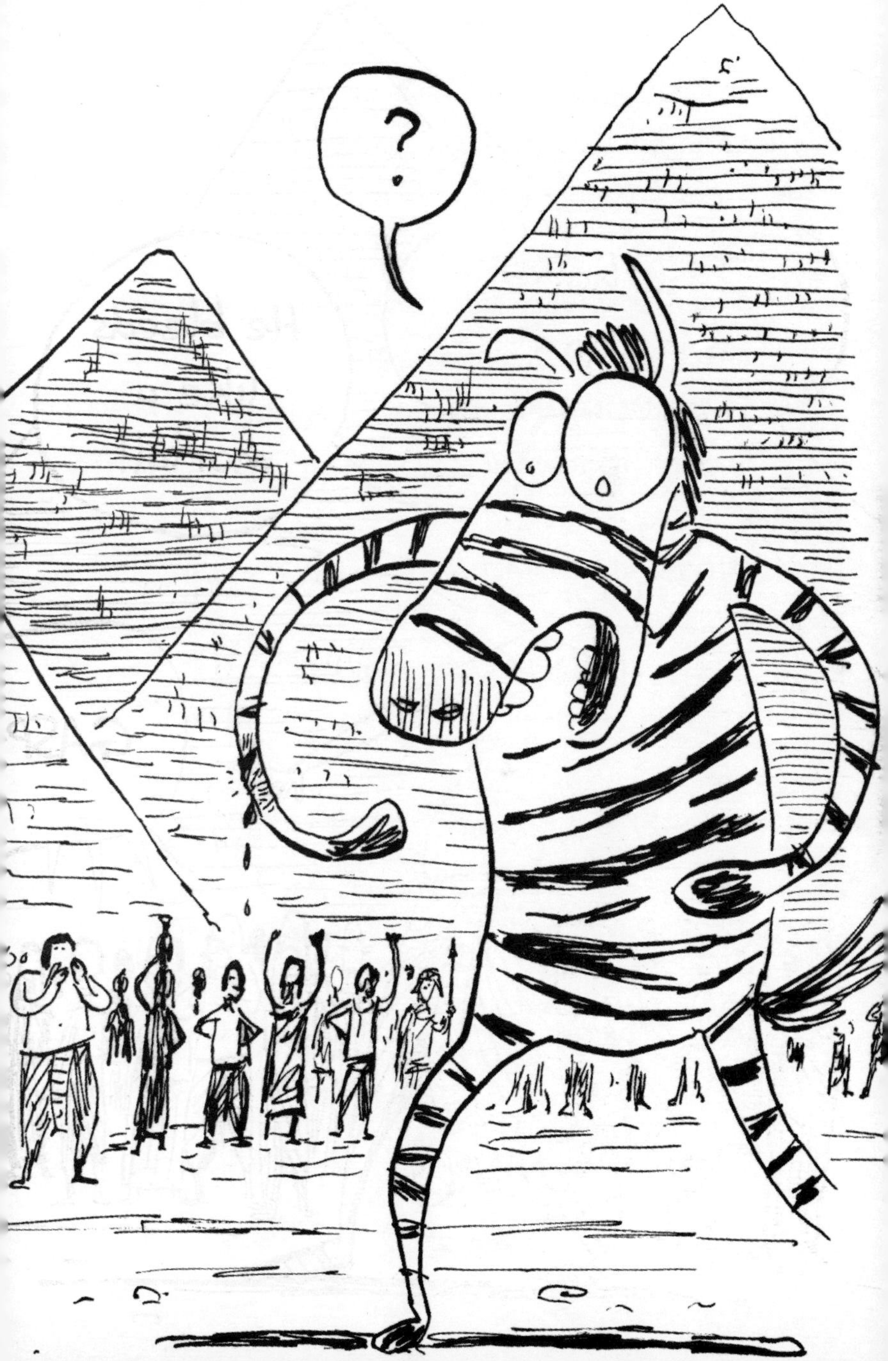
?

Julius was confused. "Wait ... what?" He looked over his body to see where he'd been injured.

Cornelius grabbed him by the arm. "It's your elbow. You've cut your elbow!"

"Yeah, so?" Julius didn't understand why it was such a big problem to have a graze.

"Gods DON'T bleed, Julius," Cornelius told him. "It said so in those old scrolls I read. The game is truly up."

The restless crowd began to surge towards Julius and his friends.

"We've all had it!" panicked Julius.

"Not necessarily!" cried out Lucia.

Help us lift this thing up!

It's still in one piece!

They all rushed over to help lift the chariot, which tipped back onto its wheels with a huge CRASH!

Julius gazed at the unbroken chariot with relief. "Maybe our luck has changed after all!"

Milus grabbed the antelope and shoved him on the chariot. "If you don't button it, I'll make you wish you'd never set eyes on that rotten rock!"

CHAPTER NINETEEN
WHEEL OF FORTUNE

Julius and Brutus quickly grabbed hold of the reins just as Imhotep and his guards approached.

"STOP THEM!" bellowed the priest as he realized what they were doing. "THEY'RE GETTING AWAY!"

With everyone on board, the two zebras dashed off, bashing their way through the crowds.

The chariot quickly zoomed away from the pyramids and the angry mob, heading off along the riverbank.

Lucia quickly steered them onto a smoother road that led towards a range of hills. "Hold on tight!" she said. "Once we get past those hills, we'll be well on our way out of this place!" She turned to Rufus to give him a high five, when there was a sudden great CLUNK underneath the chariot.

The chariot and all its passengers tumbled down the riverbank in a crunching, screaming cloud of dust.

As everybody hauled themselves up and dusted themselves down, Julius spotted Felix rummaging through the wreckage. The antelope pulled out his prized gem and polished it with his hoof. "Phew!" he gasped. "I thought I'd lost it!"

Felix tried to grab it back. "IT'S NOT CURSED!" he wailed. "IT'S NOT MY FAULT YOU'RE STUPID AND UNLUCKY!"

Milus grabbed the gem out of Julius's hoof. "The goat is right, for once," he growled. "You've always been a clumsy nincompoop, gem or no gem."

But Cornelius wasn't having any of it and snatched the gem from Milus's paw.

"No no no NO! You don't UNDERSTAND!" he said. "Pharaohs' curses aren't just fanciful fairy tales. THEY'RE REAL!"

"YEAH! EVERYTHING has gone wrong since you turned up with this jinxed gem!" Julius agreed.

"Now, anything that COULD go wrong, DOES go wrong!" Julius said, sitting down in a huff.

Lucia suddenly leapt to her feet. "Seriously!" she cried. "That stone IS cursed!" She pointed down the river, fear in her eyes.

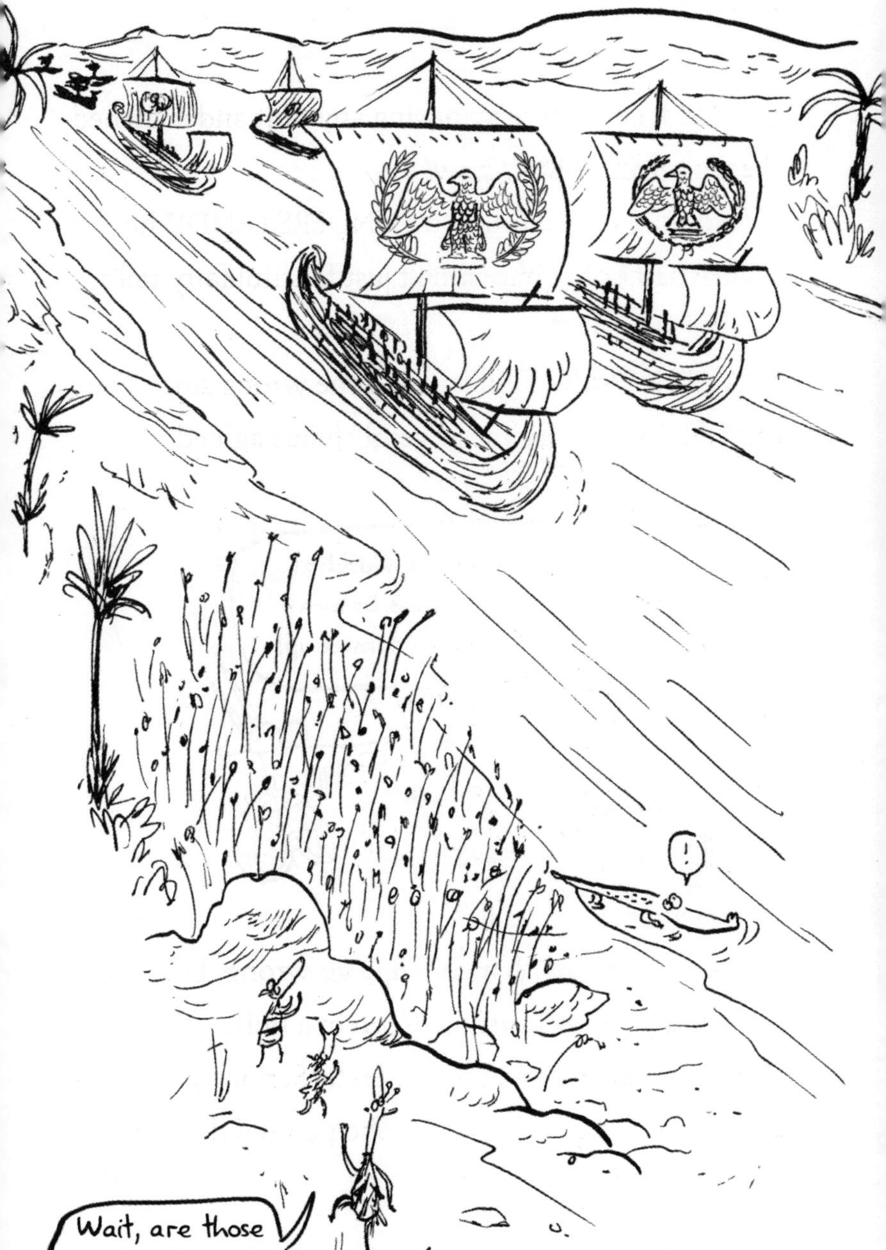
!
Wait, are those ROMAN ships?!

"And if I'm not very much mistaken, that is the crest of HADRIAN himself!" observed Cornelius in alarm.

"HADRIAN?!" blurted Pliny. "What's that loser doing in EGYPT?"

"WHO CARES!" spluttered Julius.

Abandoning the wreckage of the chariot, the animals headed towards the hills as fast as their legs could carry them. As they ran, Julius turned to Felix.

"I don't care what you say, Felix!" he panted. "We're putting that gem back, WHETHER YOU LIKE IT OR NOT!"

CHAPTER TWENTY
I WANT MY MUMMY!

Milus raised his paw. "Could someone please remind me why we're dressing up in old bandages?"

Poor Lucia was becoming quite exasperated at having to explain everything again.

It's a DISGUISE, MILUS!

"Egyptians wrap their dead bodies in bandages so they'll be nicely preserved for their journey to the underworld!"

Felix put up his hoof. "Does that mean we'll be going to the underworld, now we're dressed as mummies?"

"But won't people be freaked out by seeing mummies wandering around?" asked Julius as he wrapped the last bit of bandage around his face.

"No, no. Mummies are quite common," replied Lucia breezily. "It's perfectly normal!"

Lucia clapped her claws to get everyone's attention. "So, do we all understand the plan? We sneak into Cleopatra's tomb, return Felix's cursed stone, then head back home before anyone notices. Simple!"

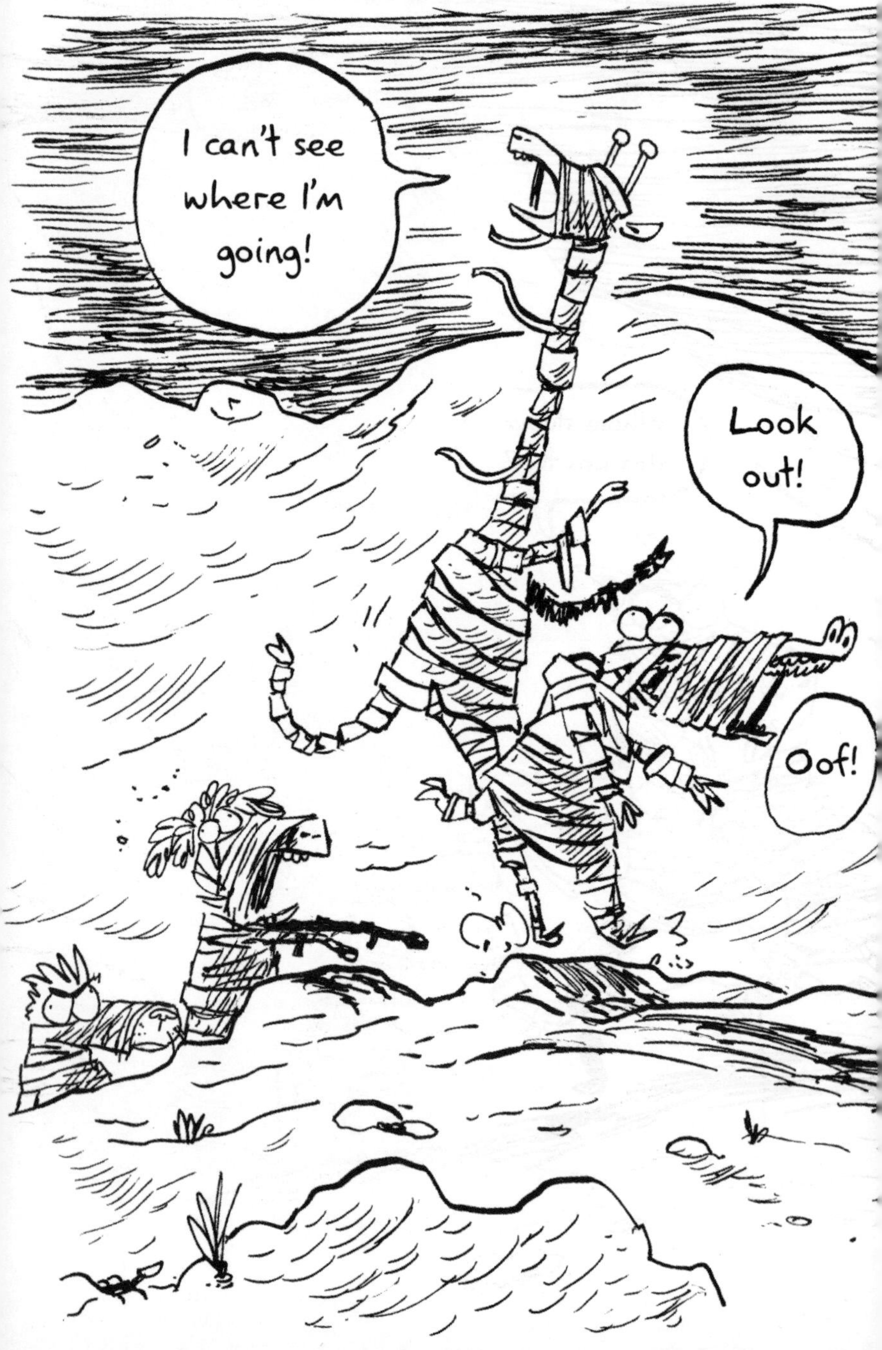
I can't see where I'm going!
Look out!
Oof!

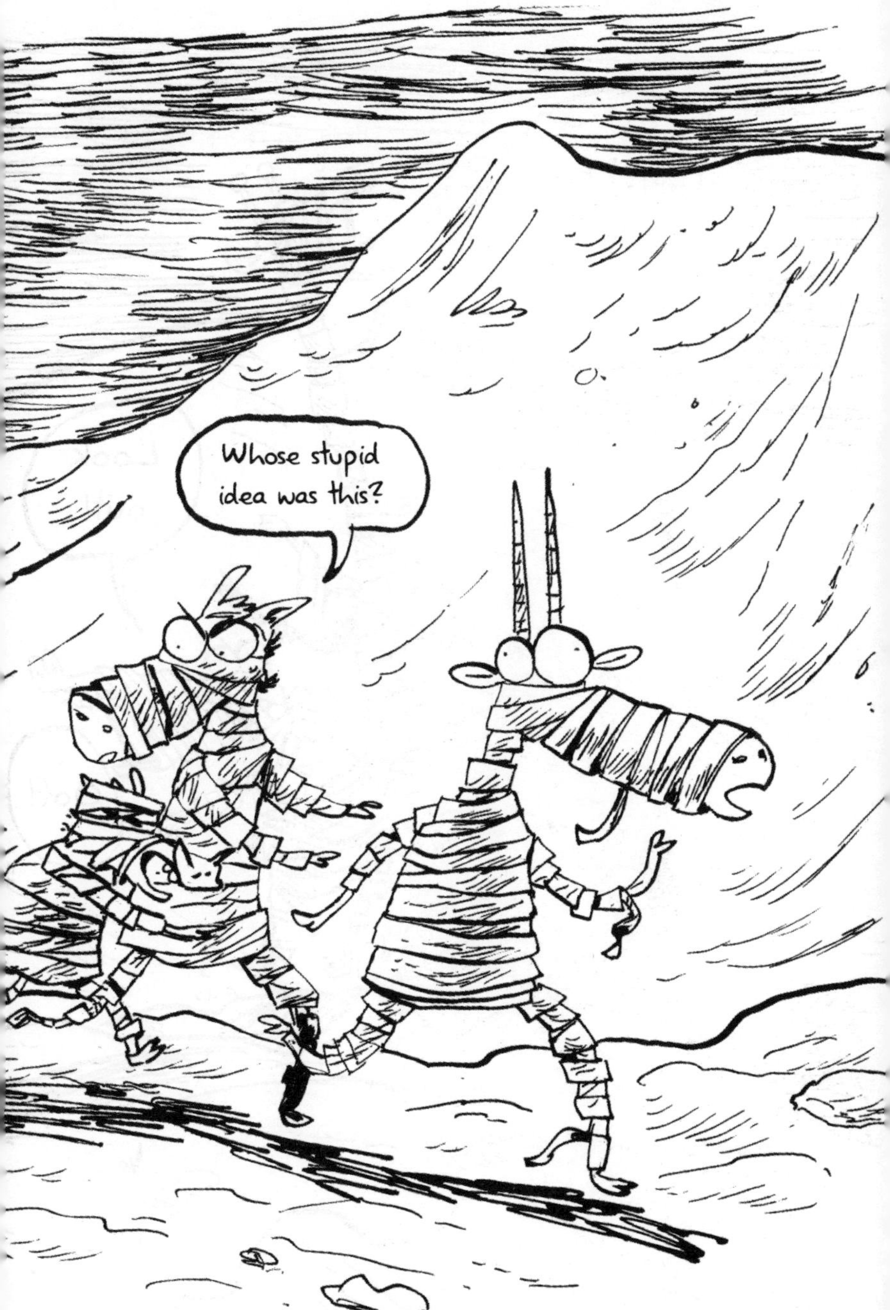
Whose stupid idea was this?

As they fumbled their way through the rocky outcrops, Julius grabbed Felix and jostled him to the front. "You'll have to show us the way. I've only been there once!"

But all these rocks look the same!

Cornelius trotted up to join them. "Wasn't there a tiled floor that led to the tomb?"

"Oh, yes!" laughed Felix in relief. "Well remembered, Cornelius. It was also only a short walk from the big statue of Heter. So we need to make sure that's nearby!"

Julius lifted up the bandage from his face to have a peek. "We're not too far away. Look, there's the statue!" He pointed to the enormous familiar figure of Heter ahead.

"Excellent!" said Felix, groping the walls. "Then it must be right round here somewhere..."

Suddenly, there was a sharp whistle.

Everyone immediately stuck their arms out in front of them and made weird groaning and gurgling noises.

Julius peeked out from under his bandage again. "Did it work? Did we manage to sneak past them?"

Milus yanked his bandage off his face and threw it on the ground.

"Well, if you call running away and screaming a success, then yes, our disguises completely worked."

"Let's just hope he doesn't tell anyone," worried Cornelius. "In my opinion, a bunch of idiots running around dressed as mummies is bound to raise suspicion."

As they carried on walking along the rocky valley, Felix stopped and started tapping his hoof on the ground. "'Ere, Cornelius, check this out."

"Good work, Felix!" praised Cornelius. He turned
to the rest of the group. "This is it! Quickly, down
these steps!"

Everyone tumbled through the heavy doors into the pitch-black chamber.

"Felix!" shouted Julius. "Turn your lamp on!"

For a few, very long seconds, everyone sat quietly in the dark. There was a faint scratching noise and the tiniest of sparks flew into the air then disappeared. Finally, Felix's face lit up as the flame from his lamp burned brightly.

"'Uh-oh' what?" asked Julius, concerned.

"Well," replied Felix, "either someone's cleaned this place out and scrubbed all the walls, or we're in the wrong tomb."

"WRONG TOMB?!" gasped Julius.

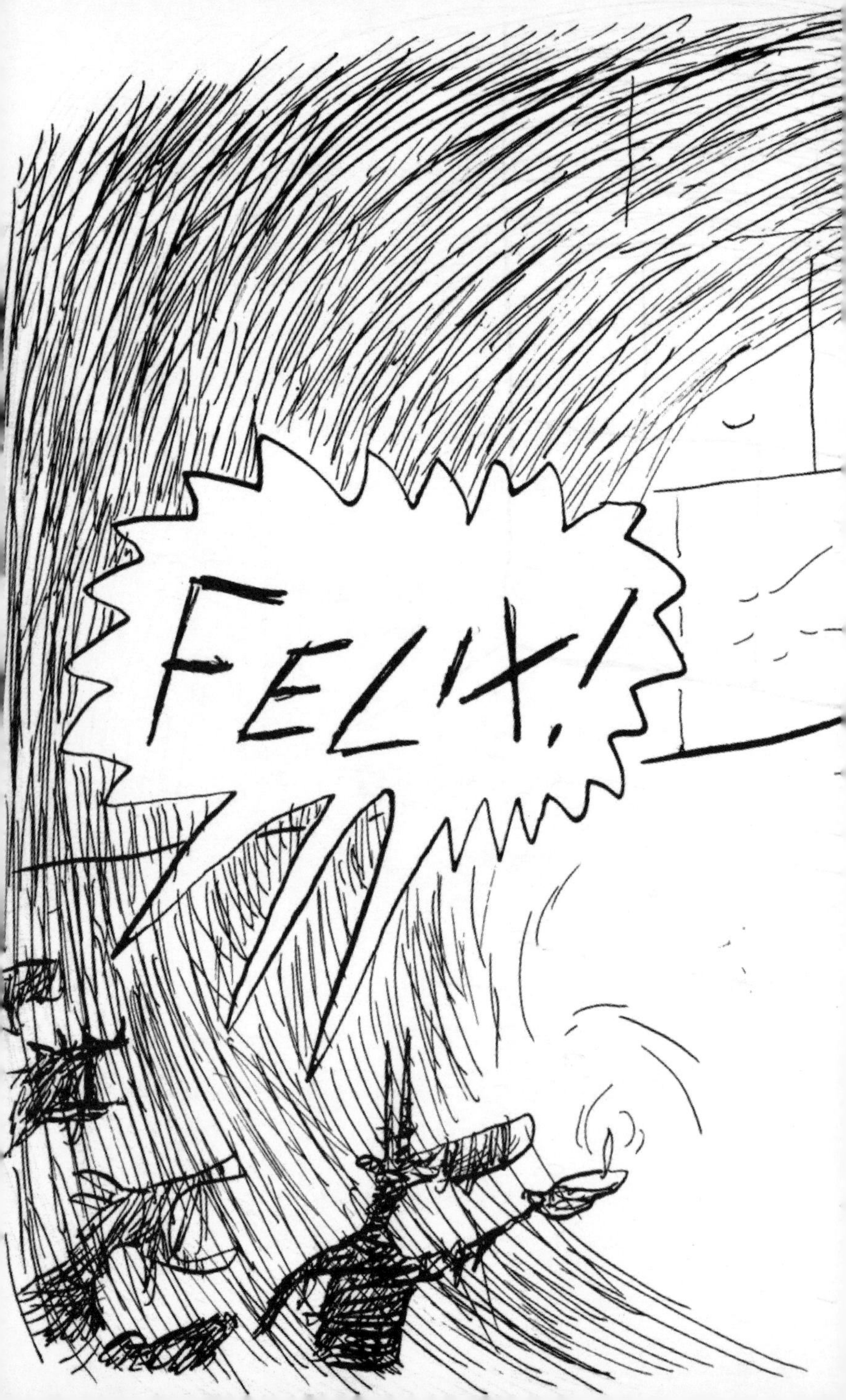
FELIX!

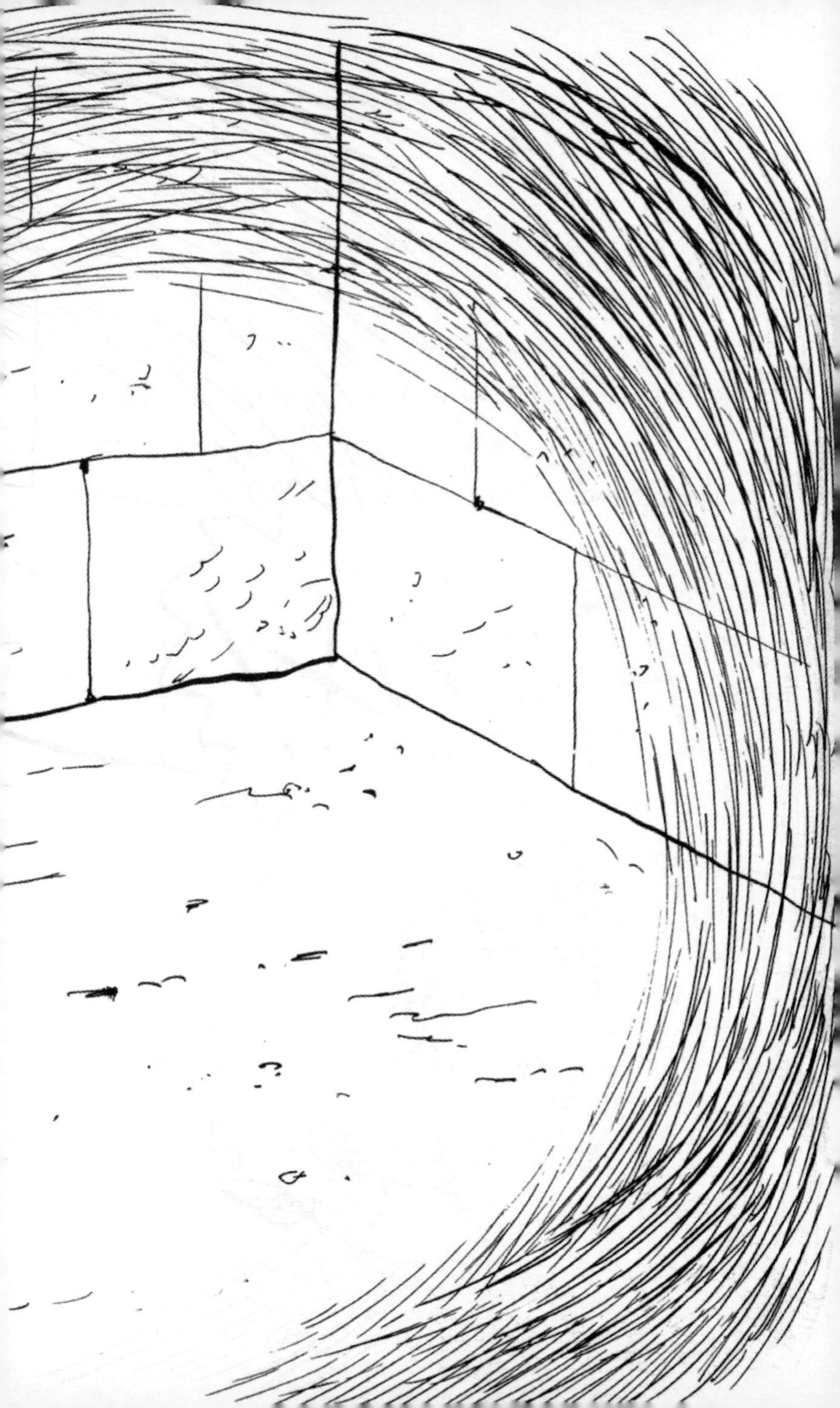

"You absolute BONEHEAD!" shouted Julius.

Everyone got to their feet and dusted themselves down.

"Can't we just leave the stone here?" suggested Brutus hopefully. "No one's going to notice, right?"

"No, Brutus!" replied Cornelius. "We need to return this to its rightful place, or we'll NEVER break the curse."

As they all made their way back to the doorway, Felix skipped to the front. "I bet it's just next door!" he laughed. "We'll be off home before you know it!"

But as Felix went to squeeze between the stone doors, he found a mysterious figure blocking his way.

The irate priest stood motionless in the doorway. "Yes, it is I!" he declared. "Word reached me of a group of animals dressed as mummies and I knew it had to be you."

Your discarded bandages led me directly to this tomb.

He tossed them into Julius's face. "YOU, foul vermin," cried Imhotep, pointing at the zebra. "YOU have defrauded an ENTIRE NATION!"

Brutus pushed himself in front of Julius. "Don't you DARE talk to my brother like that!" he said, waving his hoof menacingly.

But Imhotep was not to be silenced. He raised his arms aloft. "Step back, imbecile. YOU ARE ALL CULPABLE FOR THIS DECEPTION!"

And for that, the sentence is DEATH!

Before anyone could react, the priest stepped back and he and his guards slammed the heavy stone doors shut with a great THUD!

"HE'S SEALED US IN!" screamed Julius, and they all rushed to the doors and tried to claw them open.

But it was too late.

Imhotep had entombed them for ever.

CHAPTER TWENTY-ONE

MEET THE BEETLES

"This is all your fault, Felix!" gasped Julius. "Your precious stone has worked its wonders YET again!"

Felix stepped away from the doors and hugged his knapsack tightly to his body. "Now, just wait a minute…" he stammered.

"Wait a minute NOTHING!" roared Milus. He leapt at Felix and ripped the knapsack out of his hooves. "You were given enough chances, foolish goat! Now look at the mess you've got us in!"

Felix pushed Milus off and stepped even further back. "Look, I'm sure we can find another way out. Can't Pliny squeeze through a gap under the doors or something?"

"I could try one of my spanking new fighting moves, though!" Pliny declared excitedly. He stood well back, then threw himself head first at one of the stone doors.

Cornelius confronted Felix. "There's no way out, you idiot!" he raged. "We're entombed! There's no escape! THIS IS WHERE WE DIE!"

As they gloomily began discarding the rest of their bandages, Felix's lamp flickered, as if a gust of air had blown past.

"Well, my angry friends, that's not entirely true!" came a tiny voice.

Everyone turned to look at Pliny.

"What do you mean by that?" Julius asked the little mouse.

"Eh?" exclaimed Pliny. "How rude! That wasn't me!" He glanced at Milus. "I don't have a squeaky voice like that, do I?"

The little voice squeaked again. "NO! It wasn't him with the big hairy ears!"

It was I, Khepi!

"Cor! A little beetle!" Julius said, and he bent down to have a closer look. "Peeyoo! What's that rotten smell?"

"Anyway," continued the little beetle chirpily, "I am here to tell you that you are NOT actually to be entombed here for ever and that, in fact, you can be free! Isn't that nice?"

Everyone let out a great cheer. Brutus ran over to the little beetle. "Oh, Khepi, I could kiss you!" he declared.

Khepi scampered up the wall and pushed against one of the loose blocks. "See?" he puffed. "This wall is not as it would appear!"

Julius joined him and helped push against the block, which, after a good shove, fell through to the other side.

Julius turned to his friends. "Come on, we can easily squeeze through this hole!"

As they all pushed through the gap, they found themselves in a small chamber with three different exits. "Which way now?" asked Julius.

Khepi passed a small brown ball to him.

Please hold this for me.

Khepi licked one of his hands and held it up high. "This way!" he cried and dashed off down the third tunnel.

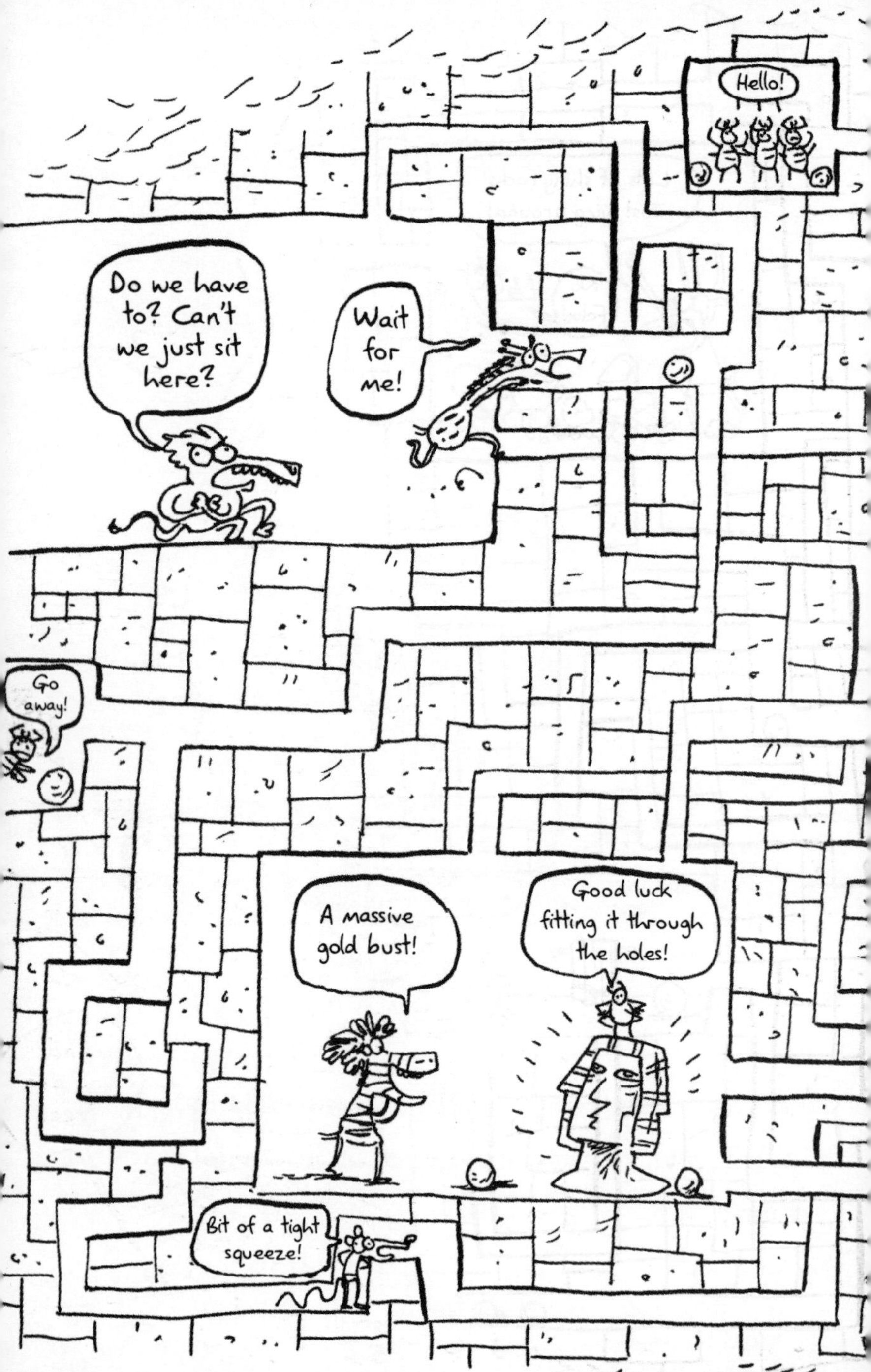
Hello!
Do we have to? Can't we just sit here?
Wait for me!
Go away!
A massive gold bust!
Good luck fitting it through the holes!
Bit of a tight squeeze!

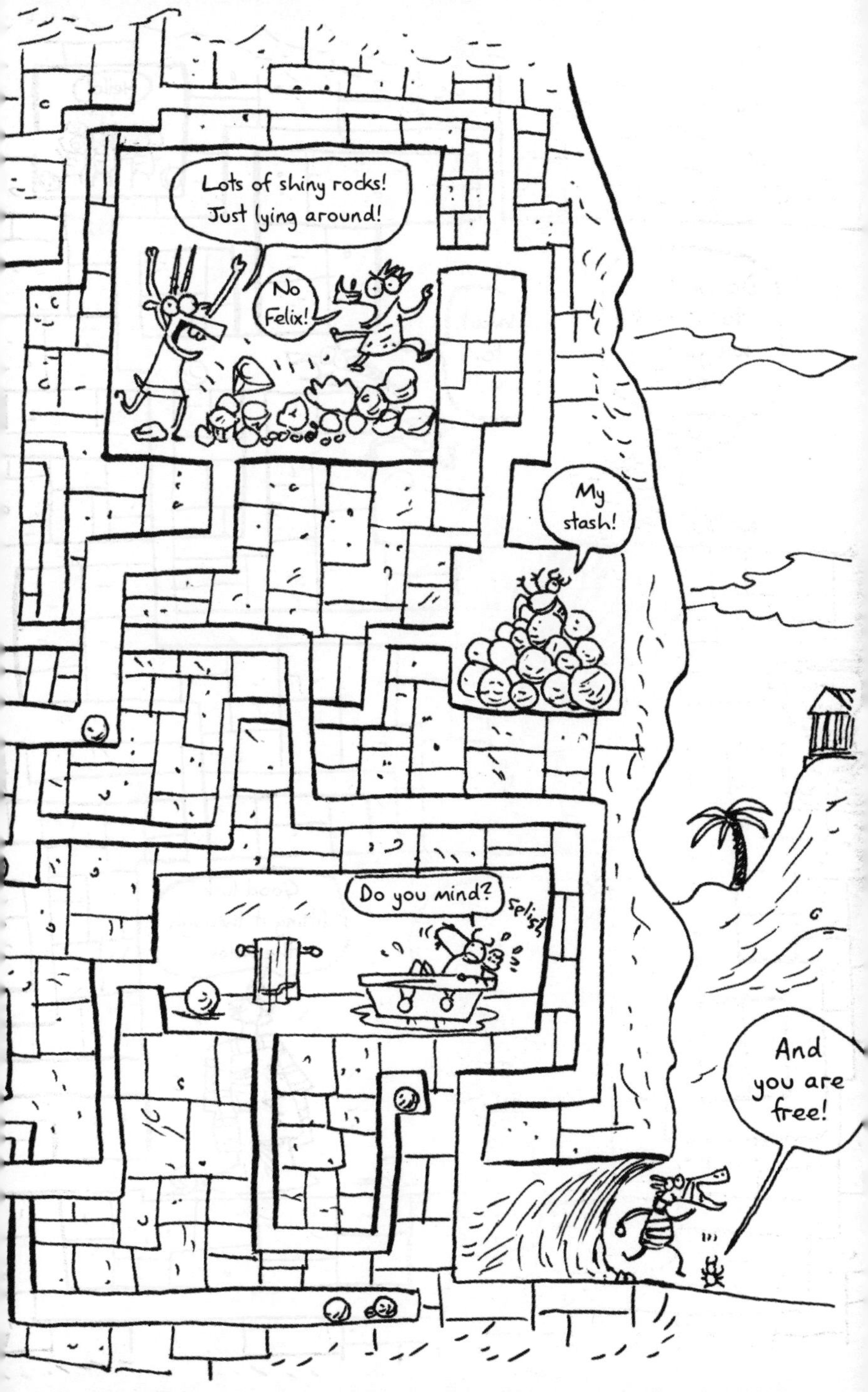
Lots of shiny rocks! Just lying around!
No Felix!
My stash!
Do you mind?
Splish
And you are free!

Finally they pushed on the last block and found themselves outside in the fresh air.

Julius crouched down beside their little beetle friend. "Thank you so much, Khepi; you've saved our lives."

It is nothing. I enjoy helping others!

"Oh, and before I forget!" Julius added. "Your little brown ball!"

"Ah! Thank you, my esteemed friend. I am eternally grateful."

Julius sniffed his hoof. "What is it anyway?"

As Julius reeled from this revelation, a loud blast of trumpets bellowed behind them.

As they all spun round, they were greeted by the sight of a small army disembarking from the great flotilla they had witnessed earlier.

"Hadrian!" whispered Julius. "Now we're REALLY for it!"

CHAPTER TWENTY-TWO
CURSE OF THE MUMMY

Julius and his friends quickly dived behind some rocks before they could be spotted. Then, slowly, Cornelius poked his head up to have a look.

"What's happening?" whispered Julius. "Did he see us?"

"I don't think so," replied Cornelius. "In fact, I'm pretty sure he's talking to someone!"

Julius stuck his head up and recognized immediately who it was. "IMHOTEP!" he cried. "And he's got a whole army with him! What's that villain saying to Hadrian?"

If you'd keep quiet, I'd be able to hear!

"WOW!" exclaimed Cornelius. "Hadrian is demanding to see YOU!"

"HE IS?!" Julius was flabbergasted. "But how did he know I was here?"

"I guess that Roman prefect must have told him." The little warthog listened intently again. "Apparently Hadrian's got a surprise for you!"

Ooh! I love surprises!

Clap!

"Uh-oh," Cornelius continued. "Imhotep has just told Hadrian that you were a false god and that you have been disposed of!"

"DISPOSED OF?!" cried Julius. "I'm not having THAT. I want my surprise!" With that he leapt up and proudly walked towards the two men.

"Julius, wait!" Cornelius called out, but it was too late.

Julius strode defiantly up to the two men.

"Morning all!" he said casually.

Imhotep's jaw nearly dropped to the floor.

"Y-YOU!!" he spluttered, barely able to believe his eyes.

Hadrian laughed. "Yet again, the zebra continues to defy and astound!"

Imhotep was still in disbelief. "HOW did you get out?" he cried. "That tomb was sealed shut from the outside. NONE could have escaped!"

Imhotep fell to his knees. "Then I beg your forgiveness, for you are truly a god among men."

Julius turned to Hadrian. "See? They think I'm PRETTY special round here. So you'd better sling yer HOOK!"

Hadrian chuckled to himself. "I'd forgotten what an impetuous little donkey you are." He put his arms behind his back and paced up and down. "Egypt is one of my favourite provinces, you know. I didn't take it too kindly when I found out you'd strolled in and assumed control."

Hadrian turned to face his ship and clicked his fingers. "So, obviously, I had to come and reclaim my beloved Egypt!"

"That's a terrible present!" complained Julius, disappointed. "You can keep him!"

Hadrian huffed in frustration. "No! NOT Septimus!" He clicked his fingers furiously. "THIS is my present!"

Septimus disappeared below deck and came back with another figure – a pathetic, tired-looking creature, shackled in chains and looking extremely unhappy. Julius strained his eyes to make out who it was silhouetted against the sun.

But then Julius realized exactly who it was. He put his hooves over his mouth as he inhaled a deep breath. "NO WAY!" he choked.

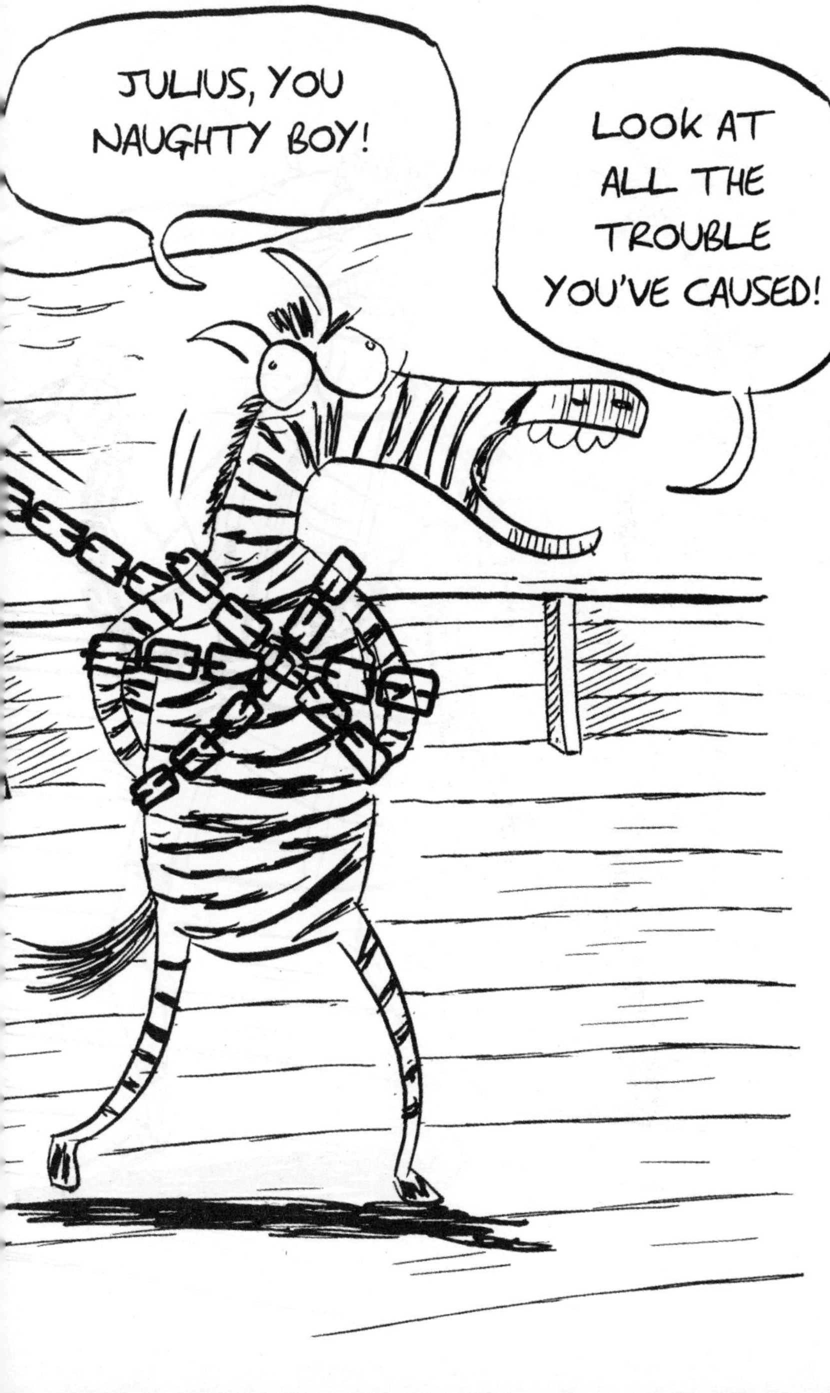
JULIUS, YOU NAUGHTY BOY!
LOOK AT ALL THE TROUBLE YOU'VE CAUSED!

"MUM!!" cried Julius. "What are YOU doing here?!"

"I am here because of YOU!"

"Yes, Julius," said Hadrian smugly. "When we discovered we had the MOTHER of our beloved champion..."

Let's just say we knew we had a valuable prize!

"And now they tell me you're PHARAOH of Egypt," said Julius's mum.

I'm angry but I'm proud of you, son.

Milus grunted under his breath. "Can someone pass me a bucket? I want to be sick!"

"I'm here too, Mum!" said Brutus, running up to stand beside Julius.

Julius's mum rolled her eyes with contempt. "YOU!" she whinnied. "Silly boy, you were meant to bring your brother BACK HOME! Look at us all now. We are in an even BIGGER mess than ever before."

Brutus hung his head in shame. "Sorry, Mum."

"And take that seaweed off your head," she barked. "You look like a FOOL!"

Yes, Mum. Sorry, Mum.

"But I am happy to see that you are still alive, Brutus. It gladdens my heart to see BOTH of you still alive."

Hadrian leapt between the zebras. "ENOUGH OF THIS PRATTLING!" he commanded, turning to Julius. "YOU!" he ordered. "Hand yourself over and give me back Egypt, or I shall throw your mother to the crocodiles!"

Julius's mum tried to free herself from her chains. "Do not listen to him, Julius. He is a hyena in a man's clothing."

But, Mum! I don't want to lose you now that I've found you again!

"YOU WON'T HAVE TO!" rang out a familiar voice.

Everyone turned round to see Lucia standing proudly on her chariot.

"LUCIA!" cried Julius.

Lucia gave Julius a knowing wink. "While you lot have been arguing, I've fixed my chariot and rustled up my OWN army!"

Hadrian laughed. "How apt!" he chuckled.

"How so?" asked Julius.

"Because, zebra, after our success with bestial gladiators, I have rustled up a special army of my own!" He clicked his fingers again at his ship.

"If you won't give up Egypt willingly, then we will fight tooth and claw to take it back!"

Hadrian turned to Julius's mum. "You, madam, called me a hyena in a man's clothing, but how will your precious boy and his pathetic army do against a LEGION OF LIONS?!"

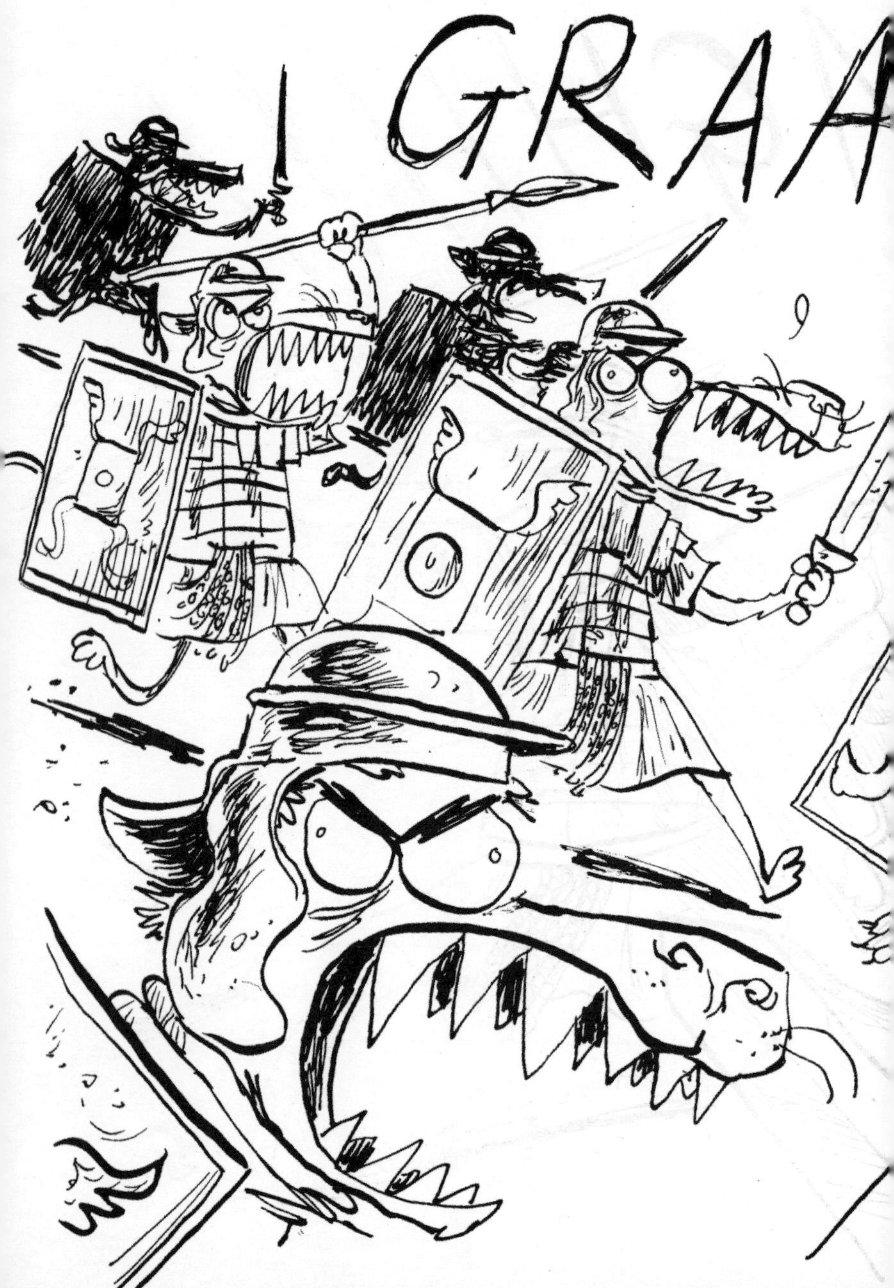
¡GRAA

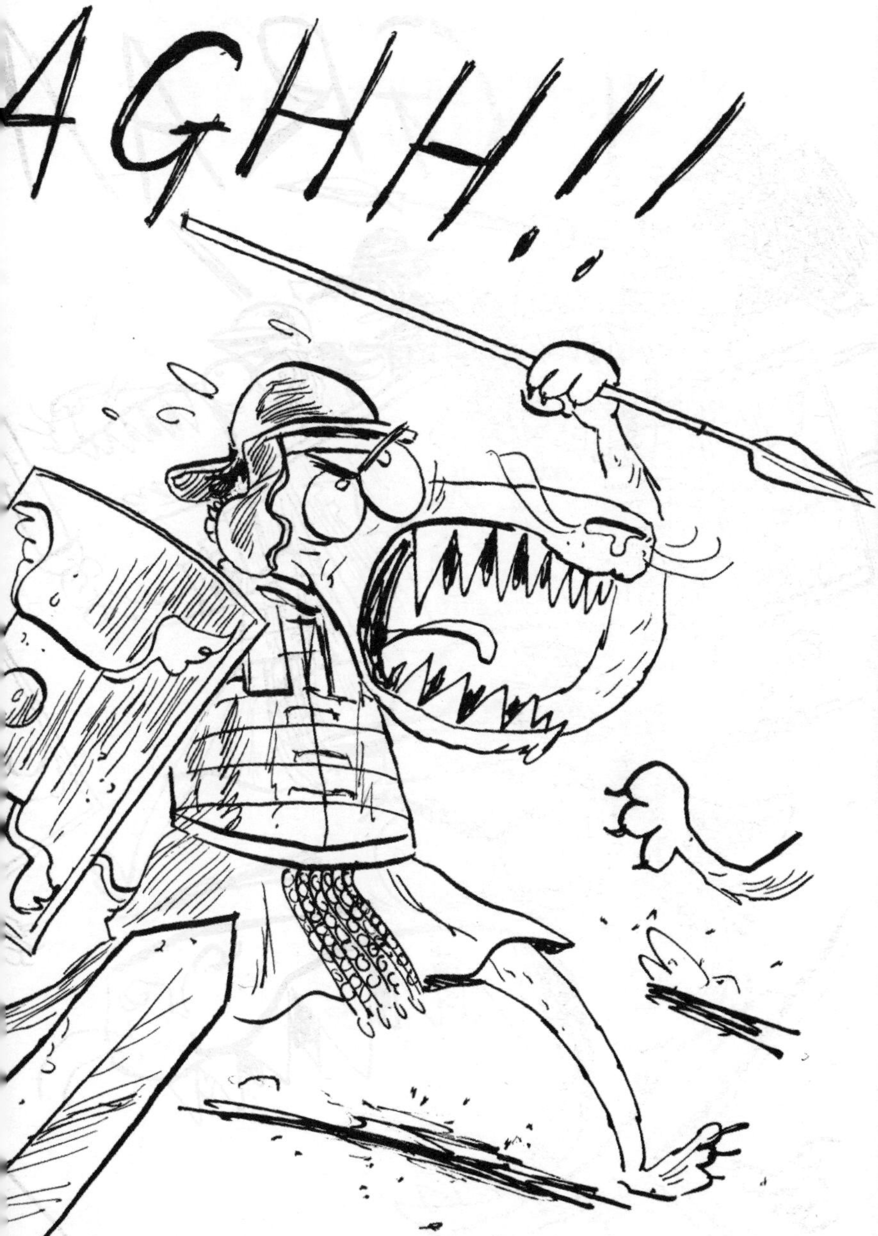
AGHH!!

CHAPTER TWENTY-THREE
CROCODILES ROCK

Imhotep's Egyptian army hurriedly passed swords and shields to Julius and his friends, and they quickly dived into the melee.

"We need to rescue Mum!" shouted Julius.

"Leave it to me!" said Brutus bravely, and he dashed towards the ship where she was being held prisoner.

Julius surveyed the rest of the battle and could see the crocodiles were easily holding their own against the lion army.

As they pushed the lions back, Julius spotted Hadrian running towards his ship.

"He knows he's lost!" Julius cried.

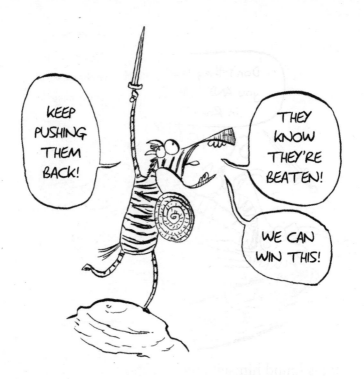

An arrow zipped past Julius's nose.

"Come down from there, you idiot!" shouted Cornelius.

A lion jumped on Julius, knocking him off the boulder. As the beast roared in his face, Julius bonked him hard on the head with his sword, knocking the lion out cold.

But no sooner had he dealt with this lion, another attacked him with a wild thrust of his sword.

Julius found himself among a group of raging crocodiles, who were grabbing lions and throwing them into the Nile. Suddenly he noticed a familiar face being held aloft, about to be chucked into the water.

"NO!" pleaded Julius. "Not that one! He's with us!"

The confused crocodile put the lion down and stormed back into the battle.

"Thank you, donkey," said Milus, brushing himself down. "I did try to tell him, but he wouldn't listen."

As the line of lions weakened, Julius headed to Hadrian's ship to find Brutus and his mother. On the deck he could see his brother tackling a Roman guard. Out of nowhere, Hadrian himself appeared. Grappling with Brutus, he threw the hapless zebra overboard. Before Julius could reach the ship, he was stopped by Felix.

"Forget about it, Felix!" cried Julius. "We've got the Romans on the run!"

Felix gestured towards Hadrian's ship. "But we wouldn't be in this mess if it wasn't for my selfishness!"

The antelope held the shining gem high in the air.
"HADRIAN!" he shouted. "I'VE GOT A PRESENT
FOR YOU!"

As Hadrian caught the gem, he lost his footing.
Reaching out a hand to steady himself, he pushed
one of his generals into the river.

There was a great thudding noise as the ship
lurched backwards, tipping everybody over on the
deck.

"WHAT SORCERY IS THIS?!" bellowed Hadrian.

Julius quickly dashed onto the stricken ship and grabbed his mother. Hadrian tried to pick himself up, but another sharp pitch sent him sprawling once more.

As he lay on the deck of his sinking ship, Hadrian called out to Julius, "Congratulations, zebra! You have beaten me again!"

JOIN ME, JULIUS! I'LL MAKE YOU A GENERAL IN MY ARMY!

TOGETHER WE CAN RULE THE EMPIRE!

Julius's mum finally threw off her chains, grabbed the emperor and dangled him high in the air. "HE'LL DO NOTHING OF THE SORT!"

CHAPTER TWENTY-FOUR
TIME TO GO HOME

As the dust settled, the last of the lions fled to their ships and set sail back to Rome, leaving the wreckage of Hadrian's royal barge as a final reminder of what had taken place that day.

Imhotep presented Julius with the Egyptian crown.

Julius patted the priest on the shoulder. "Thanks, but you keep it." Julius then thanked the crocodiles for their brilliant fighting skills. "I will never forget you, I swear."

They bowed their heads, before setting off back to the river.

"Are you ready to go?" came the voice of his mother.

"Yes, Mum. I think I've had enough of pharaohs and gods and stuff."

Even the stinky old lake seems a bit more enticing these days.

They were soon joined by Milus, Felix, Lucia, Rufus and Cornelius. "Finally!" said Milus. "We're heading home!"

Julius looked around frantically. "Wait, where's Pliny?"

He's heading back to Rome on one of the ships.

He's desperate to try out his new skills in the Colosseum.

"I'm going to miss that little mouse," sighed Julius. "Being home will seem very quiet after these last few months!"

They headed along the dusty road that stretched out in front of them. "Maybe, if I get bored, I might take Hadrian up on his job offer!" Julius chuckled. "Perhaps one day I'll rise up through the ranks to become emperor!"

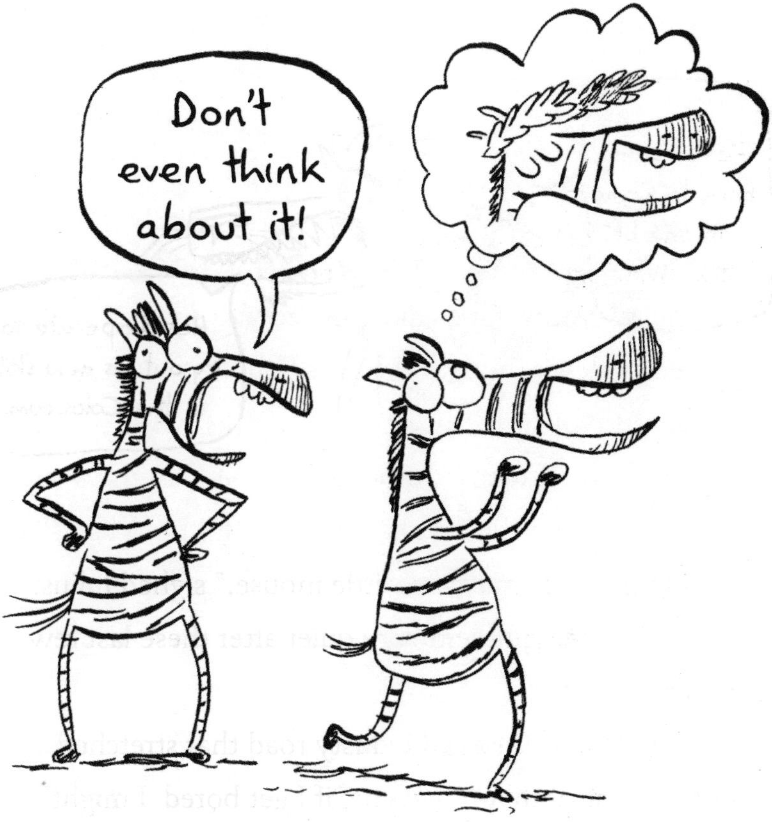
Don't even think about it!

❦EPILOGUE❦

The sun was beating down as Julius stood at the edge of the watering hole and inhaled deeply. "AH!" he sighed. "I never thought the day would come when I'd actually savour the pooey whiff of this old lake." He turned to his friends Cornelius and Milus who were also soaking up the familiar sights, sounds and smells of home. "Can you believe this is where we first met all those many moons ago? Doesn't it seem like a LIFETIME ago?"

Milus shook his head in faint despair. "And to think I only came here for a quick drink that day and ended up halfway across the world with you fools."

All I want now is a quiet life.

They bowed their heads over the lake, lapping up the cool water, when suddenly Cornelius became aware of a large man standing on the ridge opposite. The man appeared to be watching the three of them.

"Hang on," the little warthog said. "Who's the fellow in the hooded cloak? Do you recognize him, Julius?"

Julius lifted his head and squinted against the sunlight, just making out the silhouetted figure who seemed to be getting closer. Julius shook his head. "Nope," he replied. "Nothing to do with me! Shall I have a word?"

Milus quickly moved towards Julius. "Careful, donkey. I don't like the look of him!"

Without warning, the hooded stranger raced towards the lion and lunged between him and the zebra. "BEWARE, STRIPY ONE!" he bellowed. "THE BEAST SEEKS TO EAT YOU!" And, with that, the enormous man picked Milus up with his bare hands and hurled him through the air as far as the eye could see.

AAAAAAAAAAAAAA!!

"Hey! What did you do that for?" blurted Julius.

The mysterious brute flicked back his hood to reveal a round, beaming, bearded face.

I am HERACLES, son of ZEUS. I seek the champion, Julius, and his band of adventurers... And I need them all in one piece...

TO BE CONTINUED...

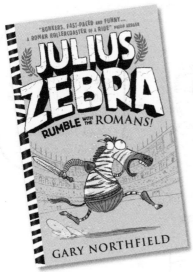

ROMAN NUMERALS

Hello readers! Julius has asked me and Felix to help explain the strange page numbers used throughout this book.

Instead of page numbers like 1, 2 and 3, you'll find V, X, I and various other letters, which are Roman numerals — just like the Romans used for counting!

Even an idiot like me can understand them. Hooray!

Here are the seven letters that represent all the Roman numerals.

I = 1
V = 5
X = 10
L = 50
C = 100
D = 500
M = 1000

Thankfully, you won't find the last two... This book is big enough as it is!

You simply add Roman numerals together to make different numbers:
II (1 + 1) = 2
VIII (5 + 1 + 1 + 1) = 8
CLI (100 + 50 + 1) = 151

That seems easy enough! I'm off to collect some rocks.

ROMAN NUMERALS

WAIT! We're not finished! There are two basic things you need to know to be able to count Roman numerals!

Oh?

1: YOU WILL NEVER FIND MORE THAN THREE ROMAN NUMERALS IN A ROW. 3 is written as III, but 4 is not IIII.

But hold on, how do you write 4 then?

My brain hurts!

2: WHEN A SMALLER NUMERAL COMES BEFORE A LARGER NUMERAL, TAKE AWAY THE VALUE OF THE SMALLER NUMERAL FROM THE BIGGER ONE TO WORK OUT THE NUMBER.

So 9 is IX?

Yes! You can remember it like this: 1 before 10 is 9.

To summarise: Always read Roman numerals from left to right, adding up as you go along. If a larger numeral comes before a smaller or equal numeral, add them together. But if a smaller numeral comes before a larger numeral, take away the value of the smaller numeral from the bigger one before moving on to the next letter in the row.

If there is a next letter, of course!

Here's some to help you along!

1 I	7 VII	13 XIII	50 L	200 CC
2 II	8 VIII	14 XIV	60 LX	300 CCC
3 III	9 IX	15 XV	70 LXX	
4 IV	10 X	20 XX	80 LXXX	
5 V	11 XI	30 XXX	90 XC	
6 VI	12 XII	40 XL	100 C	

WRITE YOUR NAME

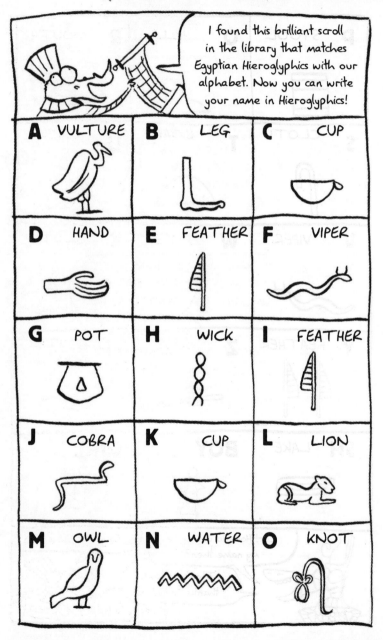

I found this brilliant scroll in the library that matches Egyptian Hieroglyphics with our alphabet. Now you can write your name in Hieroglyphics!

A VULTURE

B LEG

C CUP

D HAND

E FEATHER

F VIPER

G POT

H WICK

I FEATHER

J COBRA

K CUP

L LION

M OWL

N WATER

O KNOT

IN HIEROGLYPHICS

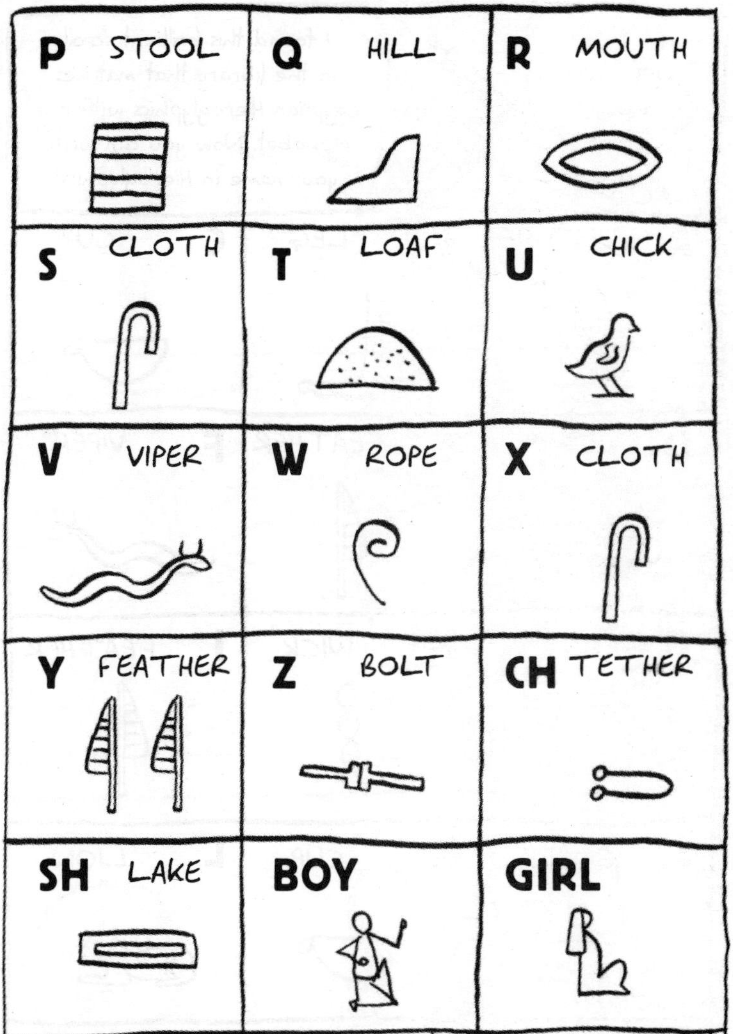

P STOOL
Q HILL
R MOUTH
S CLOTH
T LOAF
U CHICK
V VIPER
W ROPE
X CLOTH
Y FEATHER
Z BOLT
CH TETHER
SH LAKE
BOY
GIRL

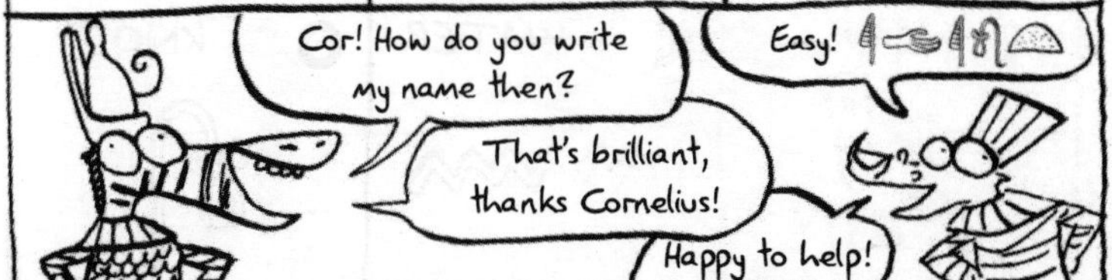

Cor! How do you write my name then?
Easy!
That's brilliant, thanks Cornelius!
Happy to help!

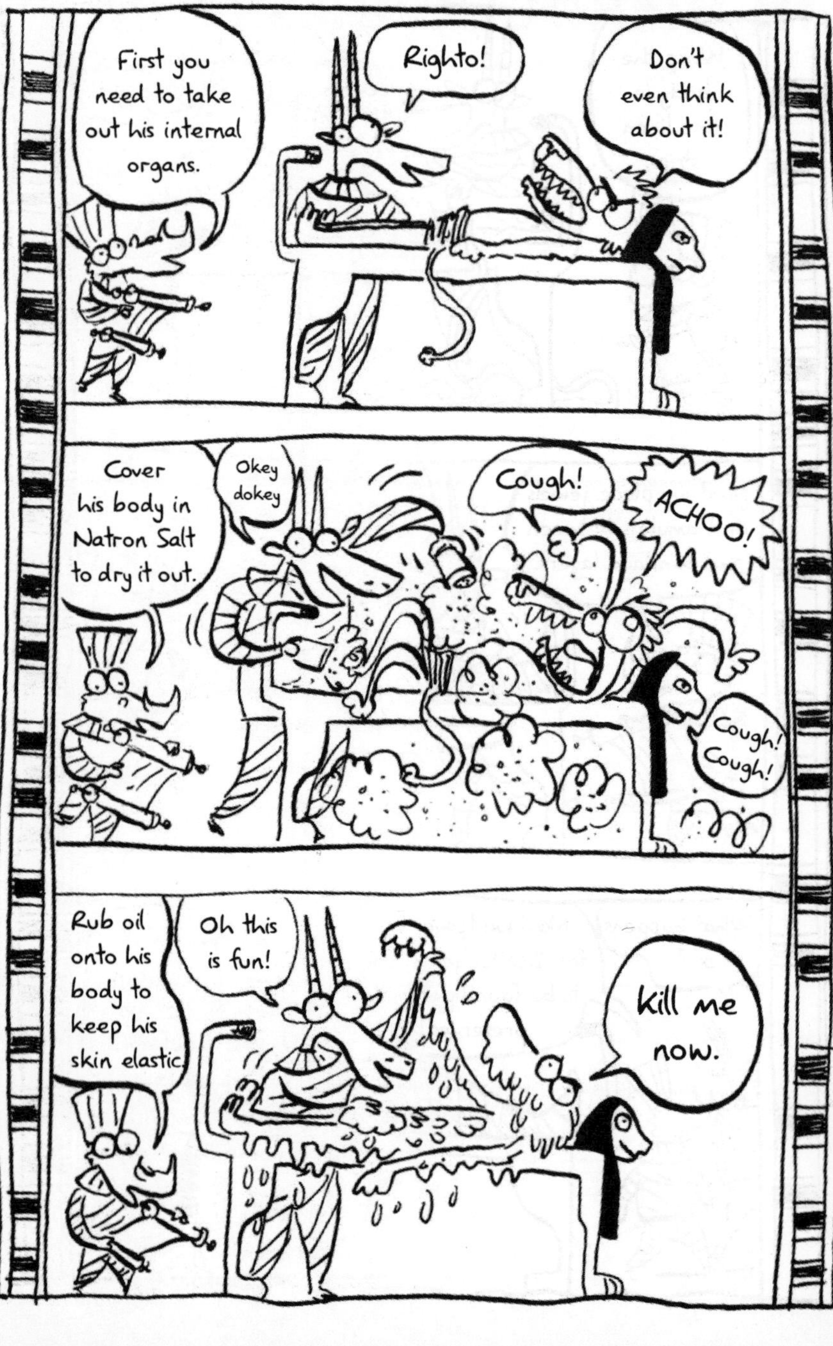
First you need to take out his internal organs.
Righto!
Don't even think about it!
Cover his body in Natron Salt to dry it out.
Okey dokey
Cough!
ACHOO!
Cough! Cough!
Rub oil onto his body to keep his skin elastic.
Oh this is fun!
Kill me now.

MUMMIFICATION

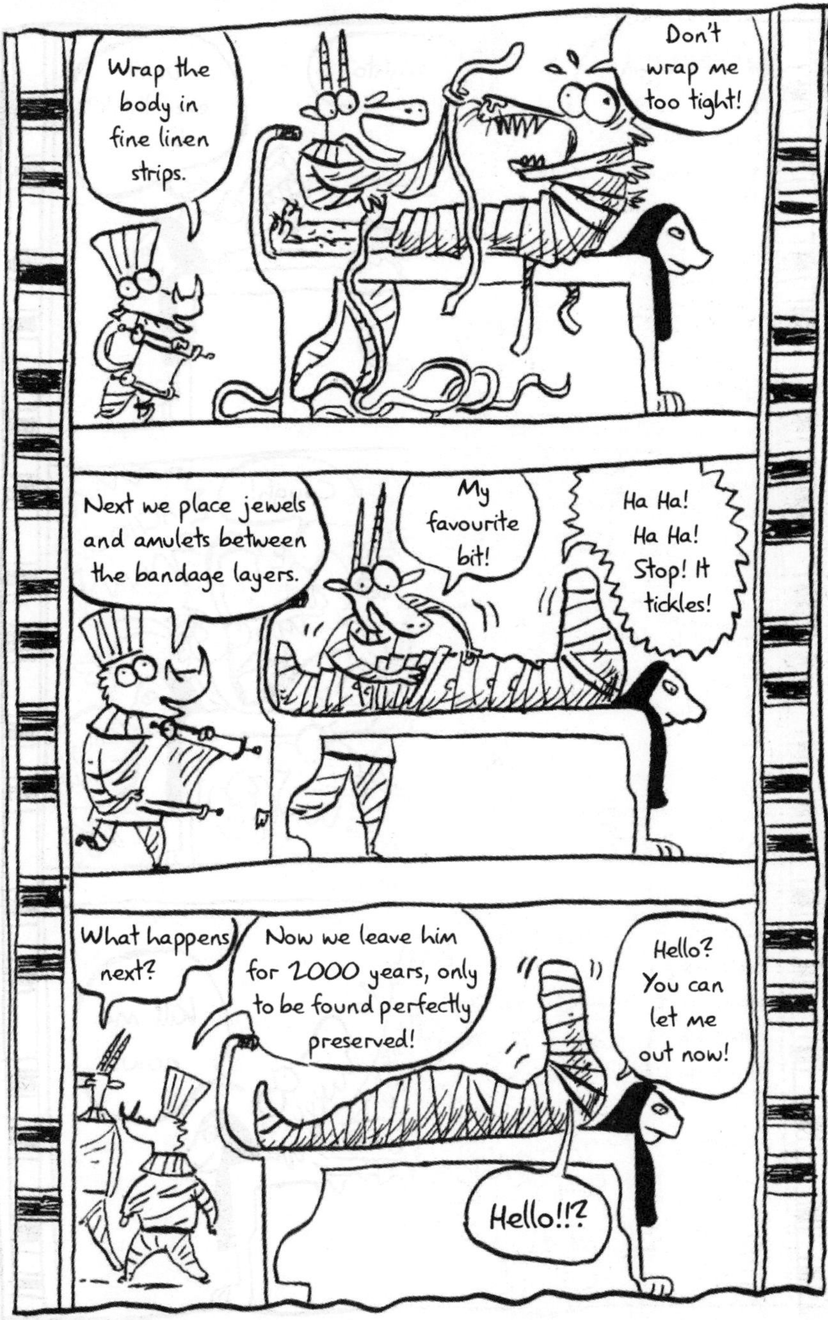
Wrap the body in fine linen strips.
Don't wrap me too tight!
Next we place jewels and amulets between the bandage layers.
My favourite bit!
Ha Ha! Ha Ha! Stop! It tickles!
What happens next?
Now we leave him for 2000 years, only to be found perfectly preserved!
Hello? You can let me out now!
Hello!!?

GARY'S GLOSSARY

ALEXANDRIA
Ancient Egyptian capital, founded by Alexander the Great in 331 BC. Had Julius continued being pharaoh, no doubt it would have been called Heteria or Julius Zebria by now.

ANCIENT EGYPTIAN DRESS
Ancient Egyptian aristocracy would show off their wealth by wearing headdresses and collars. Headdresses were made from stiff linen and often featured colourful patterns. Collars were made from precious metals such as gold, silver or copper and inlaid with gemstones. Almost all Egyptians wore wigs in an attempt to keep cool in the desert heat (though rarely seaweed), and both men and women would wear dark kohl make-up around their eyes. This make-up not only looked cool, it also provided protection for the eyes against all the desert dust that was flying around.

ANIMALS IN ANCIENT EGYPT
Ancient Egyptians believed that gods represented themselves on earth in the form of certain animals. If you were lucky enough to be a falcon, cat, hippo or crocodile, you would be worshipped and live a pampered life. Zebras, not so much.

CARTOUCHE
A long oval with a line underneath drawn around hieroglyphics to denote that the words within were a royal name. Amulets in the same shape with the pharaoh's name written on them were worn by the pharaoh and often affixed to their tomb. Also, the sound you make when you sneeze.

CLEOPATRA
Queen of Egypt and the last of the pharaohs. She married Roman dictator Mark Antony, but after losing the Battle of Actium to rival Roman leader Octavian, both Cleopatra and Mark Antony killed themselves. Their tomb remains hidden to this day.

DONKEY MILK
Renowned for its amazing rejuvenating properties, Cleopatra loved bathing in donkey's milk. It's said that 700 donkeys were needed for just one daily bath!

FIRE STRIKER
Small piece of iron shaped like a horse shoe. You would strike

it against flint or other rocks to create a spark to light your oil-soaked lamp wick, or straw tinder for your fireplace. Try not to use around libraries or temples.

GASTROMANCY

The art of interpreting the noises made by the stomach. It was believed that these noises were the voices of spirits. Interpreting them was a means of speaking to the dead and of foretelling the future, and led to the art of ventriloquism that we know and love today.

HETER

Egyptian word for a horse pulling a chariot. Normally spelt 'Htr' in hieroglyphics, alongside an image of a horse. A version of Heter was even found written in Tutankhamun's tomb. We knew Julius was special!

HIEROGLYPHICS

Form of writing using pictograms employed by the ancient Egyptians. The meaning of hieroglyphics was lost for centuries, until it could finally be translated in the early 19th Century thanks to the discovery of the Rosetta Stone in 1799.

HORUS

Earliest and one of the most important Egyptian gods. Credited with creating the sky, his right eye represents the sun and his left eye, the moon. Usually depicted as a man with the head of a bird, most likely a falcon. Or a pigeon.

THE LIBRARY OF ALEXANDRIA

Built at the beginning of the 3rd Century BC, the library of Alexandria grew to be the world's biggest, holding over half a million papyrus scrolls. It attracted the likes of important people such as Archimedes and Julius Caesar (who couldn't have been that impressed, seeing as he burnt it down in 48 BC).

MEMPHIS

Thriving capital city of ancient Egypt on the south of the Nile delta, situated in close proximity to the famous pyramids. After centuries of great prominence and importance, it fell in favour after the rise of Alexandria.

PAPYRUS

Papyrus is a material similar to thick paper, made from the pith of the papyrus plant, which grew abundantly on the banks of the Nile. Egyptians would write on papyrus in hieroglyphics and then join sections together to be rolled up into a scroll – an early form of the book!

PHARAOHS

Pharaohs were the political and religious leaders of Egypt, and were believed to be gods among men. As symbols of their deity, both male and female pharaohs would wear false beards at religious ceremonies and other important events. On such occasions, they would also carry a crook, symbolizing their kingship, and a flail, a symbol of the fertility of the land.

PHAROS

Also known as the Lighthouse of Alexandria, Pharos was one of the Seven Wonders of the Ancient World. Standing over 400ft high, it was the second tallest structure after the Great Pyramid. It was rumoured to have housed a giant mirror that could project light for 30 miles.

PRIESTS

There were many ranks of priest who all performed different roles in the temple, but the shared goal of the entire priesthood was to look after the gods. When performing religious ceremonies, priests would often wear masks to adopt the persona of a god. All priests were required to shave their heads, which in the intense Egyptian heat would definitely make them pretty grumpy!

PYRAMIDS

To protect their dead pharaohs, the Egyptians built huge triangular tombs, called pyramids. The biggest one, named the Great Pyramid, was built for Pharaoh Khufu in 2560 BC. It took around 20 years to build, using an estimated 5.5 million tonnes of limestone and hundreds of thousands of workers.

RIVER NILE

Important to the existence of Ancient Egyptian civilization, the Nile provided fertile land so crops such as wheat for food, papyrus for paper and flax for clothing could grow in an otherwise barren region. Also home to one of the world's largest reptiles, the man-eating Nile crocodile.

ROYAL BARGE

Resplendent in gold and purple silks, the royal barge would sail up the Nile, smelling of the most glorious flowers and accompanied by the relaxing music of flutes, pipes and lutes. All would flock to the riverbanks to witness such a wonder, mesmerised by the pharaoh's magnificent poop.

SARCOPHAGUS

A large stone coffin into which the bodies of dead Egyptians were placed after they had been mummified. The sarcophagi of important pharaohs and aristocrats were often adorned with elaborate carvings and hieroglyphics signalling who was inside.

SCARAB BEETLE

These little beetles that roll balls of dung were considered sacred by the ancient Egyptians. It was said that the way the beetle rolled their ball across the ground resembled how the sun was rolled across the sky, and so the morning sun god, Khepri, was named after them.

SERAPEUM

The largest and most magnificent of all the temples in Alexandria, dedicated to the god Serapis, who was the protector of the city. The temple was home to the Oracle, a wise person blessed with the power of seeing into the future – with the help of the gods, of course.

TITUS FLAVIUS

Titus Flavius Titianus was the prefect of Egypt, one of the largest provinces of the Roman Empire and the special private domain of the emperor himself. In charge of the finances of the province, prefects were appointed personally by the emperor.

TOMB RAIDERS

No sooner had a king or queen been buried than robbers would sneak in to steal their treasure. Some pharaohs tried protecting their tombs with curses, which would usually take the form of a terrible disease or a sudden attack by crocodiles, or by creating elaborate and confusing tunnels. Their efforts were usually in vain, as the robbers got in anyways.

Gary Northfield is an award-winning and bestselling author and illustrator of children's books and comics. His bestselling Julius Zebra series has now been translated into several languages worldwide and *Julius Zebra: Rumble with the Romans!* won the 2017 Spellbinding Book Award voted for by children. Gary's other books include *The Terrible Tales of the Teenytinysaurs!* (Walker) and *Gary's Garden* (David Fickling) which was nominated for the British Comic Awards. Gary's work is also published in *The Beano*, *The Dandy* and *National Geographic Kids* among many other magazines. He lives with his dog Stan and partner Nicky and together they have launched Bog Eyed Books, a showcase for UK comics. Find Gary online at www.garynorthfield.com, on Twitter as @garynorthfield and Instagram as @stupidmonster.

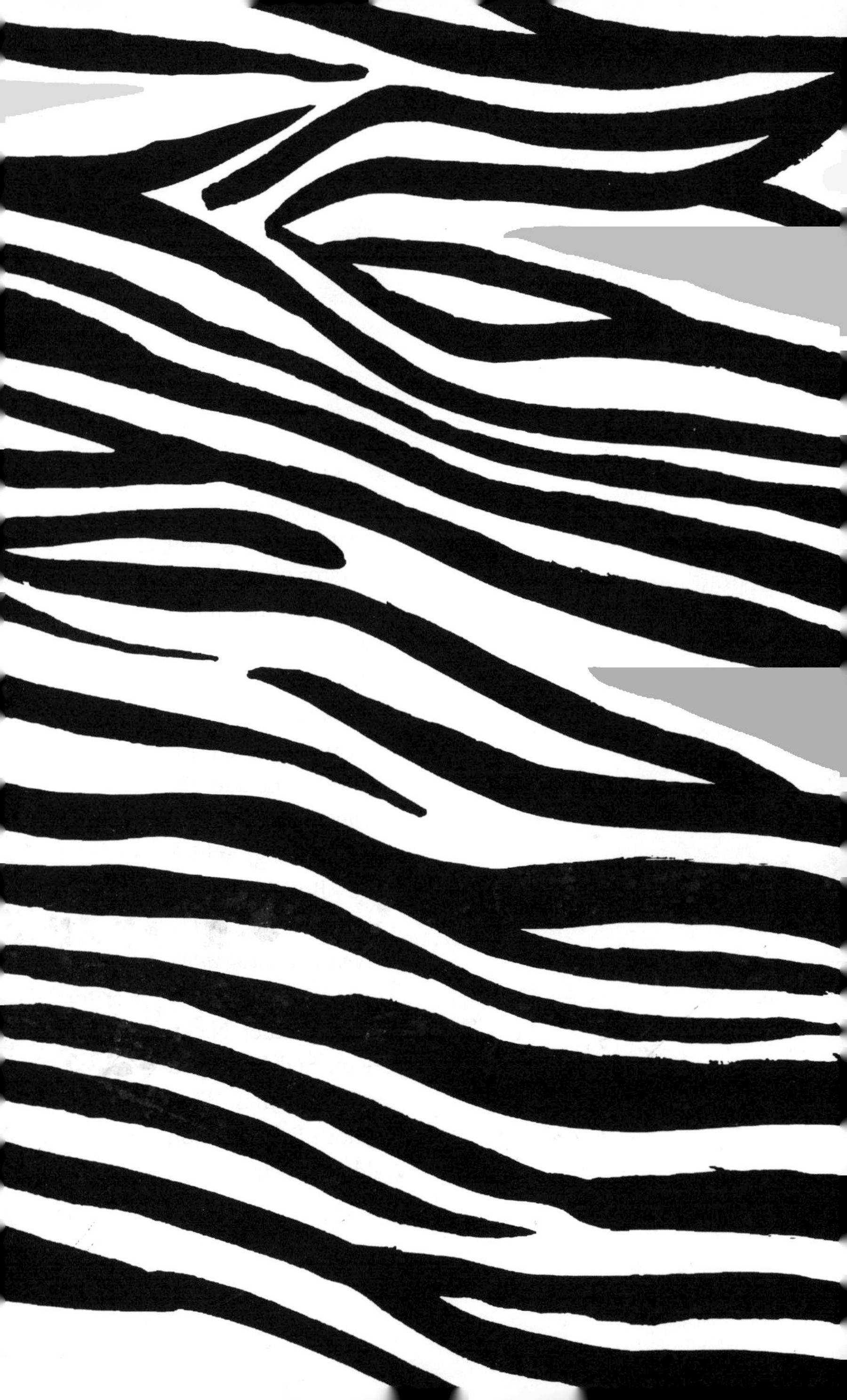